THE EA~~RT~~ ~~H~~
THE AP~~OCALYP~~SE

It was thought to have been a planetary disaster whose roots could be traced all the way into outer space. Earth had gone through a cataclysmic change and one side of the planet, like its moon, was now perpetually facing the sun. The great civilizations of Earth had nearly been destroyed, and the few survivors who remained had fallen back to primitive ways. However, the men of Killorn held a weapon that none others had…the pipe of the Gods. This fantastic instrument spelled death for any enemy who stood against it.

Master sci-fi author Poul Anderson spins a science fantasy tale of Earth in the far future. It is the story of the Men of Killorn, and how their leader, Red Bram, led them against the glowing-eyed hordes of the Genasthi, who had invaded from the lands of perpetual darkness; and how Kery, son of Rhiach, played the pipe of the gods once more.

FOR A COMPLETE SECOND NOVEL, TURN TO PAGE 75

CAST OF CHARACTERS

KERY
He was destined to become keeper of the pipe of the gods. But that day would come sooner than expected—would he be ready?

QUEEN SATHI
She was young, beautiful, and fair with her subjects. But was she an experienced enough leader to handle a full-blown war?

BRAM
This warrior chief led his force of Killornian warriors into the southlands looking for new lands, only to find the wages of war.

JONAN
He was the top general of Ryvan City and a close adviser to Queen Sathi, whom he loved. But could she trust his loyalty?

RHIACH
He was the only man on Earth to know the secret of the pipe of the gods—a weapon so powerful that armies trembled before it.

MONGKU
A Prince from the Dark Lands. If the pipe of the gods fell into his hands the world of light could very well tremble at his might.

SWORDSMAN OF LOST TERRA

By
POUL ANDERSON

ARMCHAIR FICTION
PO Box 4369, Medford, Oregon   97501-0168

CHAPTER ONE

Now it must be told of those who fared forth south under Bram the Red. This was the smallest of the parties that left Killorn, being from three clans only—Broina, Dagh, and Heorran. That made some thousand warriors, mostly men with some women archers and slingers. But the pipe of the gods had always been with Clan Broina, and so it followed the Broina on this trek. He was Rhiach son of Glyndwyrr, and his son was Kery.

Bram was a Heorran, a man huge of height and thew, with eyes like blue ice and hair and beard like a torch. He was curt of speech and had no close friends, but men agreed that his brain and his spirit made him the best leader for a journey like this, though some thought that he paid too little respect to the gods and their priests.

For some five years these men of Killorn marched south. They went over strange hills and windy moors, through ice-blinking clefts in gaunt-cragged mountains and over brawling rivers chill with the cold of the Dark Lands.

They hunted and robbed to live, or reaped the grain of foreigners, and cheerfully cut down any who sought to gainsay them. Now and again Bram dickered with the chiefs of some or other city and hired himself and his wild men out to fight against another town. Then there would be hard battle and rich booty and flames red against the twilight sky.

Men died and some grew weary of roving and fighting. There was a sick hunger within some of them for rest and a hearthfire and the eternal sunset over the Lake of Killorn. These took a house and a woman and stayed by the road. In such ways did Bram's army shrink. On the other hand most of his warriors finally took some or other woman along on the march and she would demand more for herself and her babies than a roof of clouds and wind. So there came to be tents and wagons, with children playing between the turning wheels. Bram grumbled about this, it made his army slower and clumsier, but there was little he could do to prevent it.

Those who were boys when the trek began became men with the years and the battles and the many miles. Among these was the Kery of whom we speak. He grew tall and lithe and slender, with the fair skin and slant blue eyes and long ash-blond hair of the Broina, broad of forehead and cheekbones, straight-nosed, beardless like most of his clan.

He was swift and deadly with sword, spear, or bow, merry with his comrades over ale and campfire, clever to play harp or pipe and make verses—not much different from the others, save that he came of the Broina and would one day carry the pipe of the gods. And while the legends of Killorn said that all men are the offspring of a goddess whom a warrior devil once bore off to his lair, it was held that the Broina had a little more demon blood in them than most.

Always Kery bore within his heart a dream. He was still a stripling when they wandered from home. He had reached young manhood among hoofs and wheels and dusty roads, battle and roaming and the glimmer of campfires, but he never forgot Killorn of the purple hills and the far thundering sea and the lake where it was forever sunset. For there had been a girl of the Dagh sept, and she had stayed behind.

But then the warriors came to Ryvan and their doom.

IT WAS a broad fair country into which they had come. Trending south and east, away from the sun, they were on the darker edge of the Twilight Lands and the day was no longer visible at all. Only the deep silver-blue dusk lay around them and above, with black night and glittering stars to the east and a few high clouds lit by unseen sunbeams to the west. But it was still light enough for Twilight Landers' eyes to reach the horizon—to see fields and woods and rolling hills and the far metal gleam of a river. They were well into the territory of Ryvan City.

Rumor ran before them on frightened feet, and peasants often fled as they advanced. But never had they met such emptiness as now. They had passed deserted houses, gutted farmsteads, and the bones of the newly slain, and had shifted their course eastward to get into wilder country where there should at least be game. But such talk as they had heard of the invaders of Ryvan made them march warily. And when one of their scouts galloped back to tell of an army advancing out of the darkness against them, the great horns screamed and the wagons were drawn together.

For a while there was chaos, running and yelling men, crying children, bawling cattle, and tramping hests. Then the carts were drawn into a defensive ring atop a high steep ridge and the warriors waited outside. They made a brave sight, the men of Killorn, tall barbarians in the colorful kilts of their septs with plundered ornaments shining around corded throat or sinewy arm.

Most of them still bore the equipment of their homeland—horned helmets, gleaming ring-byrnies, round shields, ax and bow and spear and broadsword, worn and dusty with use but ready for more. The greater number went afoot, though some rode the small shaggy hests of the north. Their women and children crouched behind the wagons, with bows and slings ready and the old battle banners of Killorn floating overhead.

Kery came running to the place where the chiefs stood. He wore only a helmet and a light leather corselet, and carried sword and spear and a bow slung over his shoulders. "Father," he called. "Father, who are they?"

Rhiach of Broina stood near Bram with the great bagpipes of the gods under one arm—old beyond memory, those pipes, worn and battered, but terror and death and the avenging furies crouched in them, power so great that only one man could ever know the secret of their use. A light breeze stirred the warlock's long gray hair about his gaunt face, and his eyes brooded on the eastern darkness.

The scout who had brought word turned to greet Kery. He was panting with the weariness of his hard ride. An arrow had wounded him, and he shivered as the cold wind from the Dark Lands brushed his sweat-streaked body. "A horde," he said. "An army marching out of the east toward us, not Ryvan but such a folk as I never knew of. Their outriders saw me and barely did I get away. Most likely they will move against us, and swiftly."

"A host at least as great as ours," added Bram. "It must be a part of the invading Dark Landers who are laying Ryvan waste. It will be a hard fight, though I doubt not that with our good sword-arms and the pipe of the gods we will throw them back."

"I know not." Rhiach spoke slowly. His deep eyes were somber on Kery. "I have had ill dreams of late. If I fell in this battle, before we won...I did wrong, son, I should have told you how to use the pipe."

"The law says you can only do that when you are so old

that you are ready to give up your chiefship to your first born," said Bram. "It is a good law. A whole clan knowing how to wield such power would soon be at odds with all Killorn."

"But we are not in Killorn now," said Rhiach. "We have come far from home, among alien and enemy peoples, and the lake where it is forever sunset is a ghost to us." His hard face softened. "If I fall, Kery, my own spirit, I think, will wander back thither. I will wait for you at the border of the lake, I will be on the windy heaths and by the high tarns, they will hear me piping in the night and know I have come home...but seek your place, son, and all the gods be with you."

KERY gulped and wrung his father's hand. The warlock had ever been a stranger to him. His mother was dead these many years and Rhiach had grown grim and silent. And yet the old warlock was dearer to him than any save Morna who waited for his return.

He turned and sped to his own post, with the tyrs.

The cows of the great horned tyrs from Killorn were for meat and milk and leather, and trudged meekly enough behind the wagons. But the huge black bulls were wicked and had gored more than one man to death. Still Kery had gotten the idea of using them in battle. He had made iron plates for their chests and shoulders. He had polished their cruel horns and taught them to charge when he gave the word. No other man in the army dared go near them, but Kery could guide them with a whistle. For the men of Broina were warlocks.

They snorted in the twilight as he neared them, stamping restlessly and shaking their mighty heads. He laughed in a sudden reckless drunkenness of power and moved up to his big lovely Gorwain and scratched the bull behind the ears.

"Softly, softly," he whispered, standing in the dusk among the crowding black bulks. "Patient, my beauty, wait but a little and I'll slip you, O wait, my Gorwain."

Spears blinked in the shadowy light and voices rumbled quietly. The bulls and the hests snorted, stamping and shivering in the thin chill wind flowing from the lands of night. They waited.

Presently they heard, faint and far, the skirling of war pipes. But it was not the wild joyous music of Killorn, it was a thin shrill note that ran along the nerves, jagged as a saw, and the thump of drums; and the clangor of gongs came with it. Kery sprang up on the broad shoulders of Gorwain the tyr and strained into the gloom to see.

Over the rolling land came marching the invaders. It was an army of a thousand or so, he guessed with a shiver of tension, moving in closer ranks and with tighter discipline than the barbarians. He had seen many armies, from the naked yelling savages of the upper Norlan hills to the armored files of civilized towns, yet never one like this.

Dark Landers, he thought bleakly. *Out of the cold and the night that never ends, out of the mystery and the frightened legends of a thousand years, here at last are the men of the Dark Lands, spilling into the Twilight like their own icy winds, and have we anything that can stand against them?*

They were tall, as tall as the northerners, but gaunt, with a stringy toughness born of hardship and suffering and bitter chill. Their skins were white, not with the ruddy whiteness of the northern Twilight Landers but dead white, blank and bare, and the long hair and beards were the color of silver.

Their eyes were the least human thing about them, huge

and round and golden, the eyes of a bird of prey, deep sunken in the narrow skulls. Their faces seemed strangely immobile, as if the muscles for laughter and weeping were alike frozen. As they moved up, the only sound was the tramp of their feet and the demon whine of their pipes and the clash of drum and gong.

They were well equipped, Kery judged. They wore close-fitting garments of fur-trimmed leather, trousers and boots and hooded tunics. Underneath he glimpsed mail, helmets, shields, and they carried all the weapons he knew—no cavalry, but they marched with a sure tread. Overhead floated a strange banner, a black standard with a jagged golden streak across it.

Kery's muscles and nerves tightened to thrumming alertness. He crouched by his lead bull, one hand gripping the hump and the other white-knuckled around his spearshaft. And there was a great hush on the ranks of Killorn as they waited.

Closer came the strangers, until they were in bowshot. Kery heard the snap of tautening strings. *Will Bram never give the signal? Gods, is he waiting for them to walk up and kiss us?*

A trumpet brayed from the enemy ranks, and Kery saw the cloud of arrows rise whistling against the sky. At the same time Bram winded his horn and the air grew loud with war shouts and the roar of arrow flocks.

Then the strangers locked shields and charged.

CHAPTER TWO

THE men of Killorn stood their ground, shoulder to shoulder, pikes braced and swords aloft. They had the advantage of high ground and meant to use it. From behind their ranks came a steady hail of arrows and stones, whistling through the air to crack among the enemy ranks and tumble men to earth—yet still the Dark Landers came, leaping and bounding and running with strange precision. They did not yell, and their faces were blank as white stone, but behind them the rapid thud of their drums rose to a pulse-shaking roar.

"Hai-ah!" bellowed red Bram. "Sunder them!"

The great long-shafted ax shrieked in his hands, belled on an enemy helmet and crashed through into skull and brain and shattering jawbone. Again he smote, sideways, and a head leaped from its shoulders.

A Dark Land warrior thrust for his belly. He kicked one booted foot out and sent the man lurching back into his own ranks. Whirling, he hewed down one who engaged the Killorner beside him. A foeman sprang against him as he turned, chopping at his leg. With a roar that lifted over the clashing racket of battle, Bram turned, the ax already flying in his hands, and cut the stranger down.

His red beard blazed like a torch over the struggle as it swayed back and forth. His streaming ax was a lightning bolt that rose and fell and rose again, and the thunder of metal on breaking metal rolled between the hills.

Kery stood by his tyrs, bow in hand, shooting and shooting into the masses that roiled about him. None came too close, and be could not leave his post lest the unchained bulls stampede. He shuddered with the black fury of battle. When would Bram call the charge. How long? Zip, zip, gray-feathered death winging into the tide that rolled up to the wagons and fell back and resurged over its corpses.

The men of Killorn were yelling and cursing as they fought, but the Dark Landers made never a sound save for the hoarse gasping of breath and the muted groans of the wounded. It was like fighting demons, yellow-eyed and silver-bearded and with no soul in their bony faces. The northerners shivered and trembled and hewed with a desperate fury of loathing.

Back and forth the battle swayed, roar of axes and whine of arrows and harsh iron laughter of swords. Kery stood firing and firing, the need to fight was a bitter catch in his throat. How long to wait, how long, how long?

Why didn't Rhiach blow the skid of death on the pipes? Why not fling them back with the horror of disintegration in their bones, and then rush out to finish them?

Kery knew well that the war song of the gods was only to be played in time of direst need, for it hurt friend almost as much as foe—but even so, even so! A few shaking bars, to drive the enemy back in death and panic, and then the sortie to end them!

Of a sudden he saw a dozen Dark Landers break from the main battle by the wagons and approach the spot where he stood. He shot two swift arrows, threw his spear, and pulled out his sword with a savage laughter in his heart, the demoniac battle joy of the Broina. Ha, let them come!

The first sprang with downward-whistling blade. Kery twisted aside, letting speed and skill be his shield, his long glaive flickered out and the enemy screamed as it took off his arm. Whirling, Kery spitted the second through the throat. The third was on him before he could withdraw his blade, and a fourth from the other side, raking for his vitals. He sprang back.

"Gorwain!" he shouted. "*Gorwain!*"

The huge black bull heard. His fellows snorted and shivered, but stayed at their place—Kery didn't know how long they would wait, he prayed they would stay a moment more. The lead tyr ran up beside his master, and the ground trembled under his cloven hoofs.

The white foemen shrank back, still dead of face but with fear plain in their bodies. Gorwain snorted, an explosion of thunder, and charged them.

There was an instant of flying bodies, tattered flesh ripped by the horns, and ribs snapping underfoot. The Dark Landers thrust with their spears, the points glanced off the armor plating and Gorwain turned and slew them.

"Here!" cried Kery sharply. "Back, Gorwain! Here!"

The tyr snorted and circled, rolling his eyes. The killing madness was coming over him, if he were not stopped now he might charge friend or foe.

"Gorwain!" screamed Kery.

Slowly, trembling under his shining black hide, the bull returned.

AND now Rhiach the warlock stood up behind the ranks of Killorn. Tall and steely gray, he went out between them, the pipes in his arms and the mouthpieces at his lips. For an instant the Dark Landers wavered, hesitating to shoot at him, and then he blew.

It was like the snarling music of any bagpipe, and yet there was more in it. There was a boiling tide of horror riding the notes; men's hearts faltered and weakness turned their muscles watery. Higher rose the music, and stronger and louder, screaming in the dales, and before men's eyes the world grew unreal, shivering beneath them, the rocks faded to mist and the trees groaned and the sky shook. They fell toward the ground, holding their ears, half blind with unreasoning fear and with the pain of the giant hand that gripped their bones and shook them—shook them!

The Dark Landers reeled back, falling, staggering, and many of those who toppled were dead before they hit the earth. Others milled in panic, the army was becoming a mob. The world groaned and trembled and tried to dance to the demon music.

Rhiach stopped. Bram shook his bullhead to clear the ringing and the fog in it. "At them!" he roared. *"Charge!"*

Sanity came back. The land was real and solid again, and men who were used to the terrible drone of the pipes could force strength back into shuddering bodies. With a great shout, the warriors of Killorn formed ranks and moved forward.

Kery leaped up on the back of Gorwain, straddling the armored chine and gripping his knees into the mighty flanks. His sword blazed in the air. "Now kill them, my beauties!" he howled.

In a great wedge, with Gorwain at their lead, the tyrs rushed out on the foe. Earth shook under the rolling thunder of their feet. Their bellowing filled the land and clamored at the gates of the sky. They poured like a black tide down on the Dark Land host and hit it.

"Hoo-ah!" cried Kery.

He felt the shock of running into that mass of men and

he clung tighter, holding on with one hand while his sword whistled in the other. Bodies fountained before the rush of the bulls, horns tossed men into the heavens and hoofs pounded them into the earth. Kery swung at dimly glimpsed heads, the hits shivered along his arm but he could not see if he killed anyone, there wasn't time.

Through and through the Dark Land army the bulls plowed, goring a lane down its middle while the Killorners fell on it from the front. Blood and thunder and erupting violence, death reaping the foe, and Kery rode onward.

"Oh, my beauties, my black sweethearts, horn them, stamp them into the ground. Oh, lovely, lovely, push them on, my Gorwain, knock them down to hell, best of bulls!"

The tyrs came out on the other side of the broken host and thundered on down the ridge. Kery fought to stop them. He yelled and whistled, but he knew such a charge could not expend itself in a moment.

As they rushed on, he heard the high brazen call of a trumpet, and then another and another, and a new war cry rising behind him. What was that? What had happened?

They were down in a rocky swale before he had halted the charge. The bulls stood shivering then, foam and blood streaked their heaving sides. Slowly, with many curses and blows, he got them turned, but they would only walk back up the long hill.

As he neared the battle again he saw that another force had attacked the Dark Landers from behind. It must have come through the long ravine to the west, which would have concealed its approach from those fighting Southern Twilight Landers, Kery saw, well trained and equipped though they seemed to fight wearily. But between men of north and south, the easterners were being cut down in swathes. Before he could get back, the remnants of their host was in full flight. Bram was too busy with the newcomers to pursue and they soon were lost in the eastern darkness.

KERY dismounted and led his bulls to the wagons to tie them up. They went through a field of corpses, heaped and piled on the blood-soaked earth, but most of the dead were enemies. Here and there the wounded cried out in the twilight, and the women of Killorn were going about succoring their own hurt. Carrion birds hovered above on darkling wings.

"Who are those others?" asked Kery of Bram's wife Eiyla. She was a big raw-boned woman, somewhat of a scold but stouthearted and the mother of tall sons. She stood leaning on an unstrung bow and looking over the suddenly hushed landscape.

"Ryvanians, I think," she replied absently. Then, "Kery—Kery, I have ill news for you."

His heart stumbled and there was a sudden coldness within him. Mutely, he waited.

"Rhiach is dead, Kery," she said gently. "An arrow took him in the throat even as the Dark Landers fled."

His voice seemed thick and clumsy. "Where is he?"

She led him inside the laager of wagons. A fire had been lit to boil water, and its red glow danced over the white faces of women and children and wounded men where they lay. To one side the dead had been stretched, and white-headed Lochly of Oagh stood above them with his bagpipes couched in his arms.

Kery knelt over Rhiach. The warlock's bleak features had softened a little in death, he seemed gentle now. But quiet, so pale and quiet. And soon the earth will open to receive you, you will be laid to rest here in an alien land where the life slipped from your hands, and the high windy tarns of Killorn will not know you ever again, O Rhiach the Piper.

Farewell, farewell, my father. Sleep well, goodnight, goodnight!

Slowly, Kery brushed the gray hair back from Rhiach's forehead, and knelt and kissed him on the brow. They had laid the god-pipe beside him, and he took this up and stood numbly, wondering what he would do with this thing in his hands.

Old Lochly gave him a somber stare. His voice came so soft you could scarce hear it over the thin whispering wind.

"Now you are the Broina, Kery, and thus the Piper of Killorn."

"I know," he said dully.

"But you know not how to blow the pipes, do you? No, no man does that. Since Broina himself had them from Llugan Longsword in heaven, there has been one who knew their use, and he was the shield of all Killorn. But now that is ended, and we are alone among strangers and enemies."

"It is not good. But we must do what we can."

"Oh, aye. 'Tis scarcely your fault, Kery. But I fear none of us will ever drink the still waters of the lake where it is forever sunset again."

Lochly put his own pipes to his lips and the wild despair of the old coronach wailed forth over the hushed camp.

Kery slung the god-pipes over his back and wandered out of the laager toward Bram and the Ryvanians.

CHAPTER THREE

THE southern folk were more civilized, with cities and books and strange arts, though the northerners thought it spiritless of them to knuckle under to their kings as abjectly as they did. Hereabouts the people were dark of hair and eyes, though still light of skin like all Twilight Landers, and shorter and stockier than in the north. These soldiers made a brave showing with polished cuirass and plumed helmet and oblong shields, and they had a strong cavalry mounted on tall hests, and trumpeters and standard bearers and engineers. They outnumbered the Killorners by a good three to one, and stood in close, suspicious ranks.

Approaching them, Kery thought that his people were, after all, invaders of Ryvan themselves. If this new army decided to fall on the tired and disorganized barbarians, whose strongest weapon had just been taken from them, it could be a slaughter. He stiffened himself, thrusting thought of Rhiach far back into his mind, and strode boldly forward.

As he neared he saw that however well-armed and trained the Ryvanians were they were also weary and dusty, and they had many hurt among them. Beneath their taut bearing was a hollowness. They had the look of beaten men.

Bram and the Dagh, tall gray Nessa, were parleying with the Ryvanian general, who had ridden forward and sat looking coldly down on them. The Heorran carried his huge ax over one mailed shoulder, but had the other hand lifted in sign of peace. At Kery's approach, he turned briefly and nodded.

"Well you came," he said. "This is a matter for the heads of all three clans, and you are the Broina now. I grieve for Rhiach, and still more do I grieve for poor Killorn, but we must put a bold face on it lest they fall on us."

Kery nodded, gravely as fitted an elder. The incongruity of it was like a blow. Why, he was a boy—there were men of Broina in the train twice and thrice his age—and he held leadership over them!

But Rhiach was dead, and Kery was the last living of his sons. Hunger and war and the coughing sickness had taken all the others, and so now he spoke for his clan.

He turned a blue gaze up toward the Ryvanian general. This was a tall man, big as a northerner but quiet and graceful in his movements, and the inbred haughtiness of generations was stiff within him. A torn purple cloak and a gilt helmet were his only special signs of rank, otherwise he wore the plain armor of a mounted man, but he wore It like a king. His face was dark for a Twilight Lander, lean and strong and deeply lined, with a proud high-bridged nose and a long hard Jaw and close-cropped black hair finely streaked with gray. He alone in that army seemed utterly undaunted by whatever it was that had broken their spirits.

"This is Kery son of Rhiach, chief of the third of our clans," Bram introduced him. He used the widespread Aluardian language of the southlands, which was also the tongue of Ryvan and which most of the Killorners had picked up in the course of their wanderings. "And Kery, he says he is Jogan, commander under Queen Sathi of the army of Ryvan, and that this is a force sent out from the city which became aware of the battle we were having and took the opportunity of killing a few more Dark Landers."

Nessa of Dagh looked keenly at the southerners. "Methinks there's more to it than that," he said, half to his fellows and half to Jonan. "You've been in a stiff battle and come off second best, if looks tell aught. Were I to make a further venture, it would be that while you fought clear of the army that beat you and are well ahead of pursuit, it's still on your tail and you have to reach the city fast."

"That will do," snapped Jonan. "We have heard of you plundering bandits from the north, and have no intention of permitting you on Ryvanian soil. If you turn back at once, you may go in peace, but otherwise…"

Casting a glance behind him, Bram saw that his men were swiftly reforming their own lines. They sensed the uneasiness in the air. If the worst came to the worst, they'd give a fearsome account of themselves. And it was plain that Jonan knew it.

"We are wanderers, yes," said the chief steadily, "but we are not highwaymen save when necessity drives us to it. It would better fit you to let us, who have just broken a fair-sized host of your deadly enemies, proceed in peace. We do not wish to fight you, but if we must it will be all the worse for you."

"Ill-armed barbarians, a third of our number, threatening us?" asked Jonan scornfully.

"Well, now, suppose you can overcome us," said Nessa with a glacial cheerfulness. "I doubt it, but just suppose so. We will not account for less than one man apiece of yours, you know, and you can hardly spare so many with Dark Landers ravaging all your country. Furthermore, a battle with us could well last so long that those who follow you will catch up, and there is an end of all of us."

KERY took a breath and added flatly, "You must have felt the piping we can muster at need. Well for you that we only played it a short while. If we chose to play you a good long dirge…"

Bram cast him an approving glance, nodded, and said stiffly, "So you see, General Jonan, we mean to go on our way, and it would best suit you to bid us a friendly goodbye."

The Ryvanian scowled blackly and sat for a moment in thought. The wind stirred his hest's mane and tail and the scarlet plume on his helmet. Finally he asked them in a bitter voice, "What do you want here, anyway? Why did you come south?"

"It is a long story, and this is no place to talk," said Bram. "Suffice it that we seek land. Not much land, nor for too many years, but a place to live in peace till we can return to Killorn."

"Hmmm." Jonan frowned again. "It is a hard position for me. I cannot simply let a band famous for robbery go loose. Yet it is true enough that I would not welcome a long and difficult fight just now. What shall I do with you?"

"You will just have to let us go," grinned Nessa.

"No! I think you have lied to me on several counts, barbarians. Half of what you say is bluff, and I could wipe you out if I had to."

"Methinks somewhat more than half of *your* words are bluff," murmured Kery.

Jonan gave him an angry look, then suddenly whirled on Bram. "Look here. Neither of us can well afford a battle, yet neither trusts the other out of its sight. There is only one answer. We must proceed together to Ryvan City."

"Eh? Are you crazy, man? Why, as soon as we were in sight of your town, you could summon all its garrison out against us."

"You must simply trust me not to do that. If you have heard anything about Queen Sathi, you will know that she would never permit it. Nor can we spare too many forces. Frankly, the city is going to be under siege very soon."

"Is it that bad?" asked Bram.

"Worse," said Jonan gloomily.

Nessa nodded his shrewd gray head. "I've heard some tales of Sathi," he agreed. "They do say she's honorable."

"And I have heard that you people have served as mercenaries before now," said Jonan quickly, "and we need warriors so cruelly that I am sure some arrangement can be made here. It could even include the land you want, if we are victorious, for the Ganasthi have wasted whole territories. So this is my proposal—march with us to Ryvan, in peace, and there discuss terms with her majesty for taking service under her flag," His harsh dark features grew suddenly cold. "Or, if you refuse, bearing in mind that Ryvan has very little to lose after all, I will fall on you this instant."

Bram scratched his red beard and looked over the southern ranks and especially the engines. Flame-throwing ballistae could make ruin of the laager. Jonan galled him, and yet—well—however they might bluff about it, the fact remained that they had very little choice.

And anyway, the suggestion about payment in land sounded good. And if these—Ganasthi—had really overrun the Ryvanian Empire, then there was little chance in any case of the Killorners getting much further south.

"Well," said Bram mildly, "we can at least talk about

it—at the city."

NOW the wagons, which the barbarians would not abandon in spite of Jonan's threats, were swiftly hitched again and the long train started its creaking way over the hills. Erelong they came on one of the paved imperial roads, a broad empty way that ran straight as a spearshaft southwestward to Ryvan City. Then they made rapid progress.

In truth, thought Kery, they went through a wasted land. Broad fields were blackened with fire, corpses sprawled in the embers of farmsteads, villages were deserted and gutted—everywhere folk had fled before the hordes of Ganasth. Twice they saw red glows on the southern horizon and white-lipped soldiers told Kery that those were burning cities.

As they marched west the sky lightened before them until at last a clear white glow betokened that the sun was just below the curve of the world. It was a fair land of rolling plains and low hills, fields and groves and villages, but empty—empty. Now and again a few homeless peasants stared with frightened eyes at their passage, or trailed along in their wake, but otherwise there was only the wind and the rain and the hollow thudding of their feet.

Slowly Kery got the tale of Ryvan. The city had spread itself far in earlier days, conquering many others, but its rule was just. The conquered became citizens themselves and the strong armies protected all. The young queen Sathi was nearly worshipped by her folk. But then the Ganasthi came.

"About a year ago it was," said one man. "They came out of the darkness in the east, a horde of them, twice as many as we could muster. We've always had some trouble with Dark Landers on our eastern border, you know, miserable barbarians making forays that we beat off without too much trouble. And most of them told of pressure from some powerful nation, Ganasth, driving them from their own homes and forcing them to fall on us. But we never thought too much of it. Not before it was too late.

"We don't know much about Ganasth. It seems to be a fairly civilized state, somewhere out there in the cold and the dark. How they ever became civilized with nothing but howling savages around them I'll never imagine. But they've built up a power like Ryvan's, only bigger. It seems to include conscripts from many Dark Land tribes who're only too glad to leave their miserable frozen wastes and move into our territory. Their armies are as well trained and equipped as our own, and they fight like demons. Those war-gongs, and those dead faces…"

He shuddered.

"The prisoners we've taken say they aim to take over all the Twilight Lands. They're starting with Ryvan—it's the strongest state, and once they've knocked us over the rest will be easy. We've appealed for help to other nations but they're all too afraid, too busy raising their own silly defenses, to do anything. So for the past year the war's been raging up and down our empire." He waved a hand, wearily, at the blasted landscape. "You see what that's meant. Famine and plague are starting to hit us now—"

"And you could never stand before them?" asked Kery.

"Oh, yes, we had our victories and they had theirs. But when we won a battle they'd just retreat and sack some other area. They've been living off the country—our country—the devils!" The soldier's face twisted. "My own little sister was in Aquilaea when they took that. When I think of those white-haired fiends—

"Well about a month ago, the great battle was fought. Jonan led the massed forces of Ryvan out and caught the main body of Ganasthi at Seven Rivers, in the Donam Hills. I was there. The fight lasted, oh, four sleeps maybe, and nobody gave quarter or asked it. We outnumbered them a little, but they finally won. They slaughtered us like driven cattle. Jonan was lucky to pull half his forces out of there. The rest left their bones at Seven Rivers. Since then we've been a broken nation.

"We're pulling all we have left back toward Ryvan in the hope of holding it till a miracle happens. Do you have any miracles for sale, Northman?" The soldier laughed bitterly.

"What about this army here?" asked Kery.

"We still make sorties, you know. This one went out from Ryvan City a few sleeps past. But an enemy army intercepted us on the way. We cut our way out and shook them, but they're on our tall in all likelihood. When we chanced to hear the noise of your fight with the invaders we took the opportunity…Almighty Dyuus, it was good to hack them down and see them run!"

The soldier shrugged. "But what good did it do, really? What chance have we got? That was a good magic you had at the fight. I thought my heart was going to stop when that demon music started. But can you pipe your way out of hell, barbarian? Can you?"

CHAPTER FOUR

RYVAN was a fair city, with terraced gardens and high shining towers to be seen over the white walls, and it lay among wide fields not yet ravaged by the enemy. But around it, under its walls, spilling out over the land, huddled the miserable shacks and tents of those who had fled hither and could find no room within the town till the foe came over the horizon—the broken folk, the ragged horror-ridden peasants who stared mutely at the defeated army as it streamed through the gates.

The men of Killorn made camp under one wall and soon their fires smudged the deep silver-blue sky and their warriors stood guard against the Ryvanians. They did not trust even these comrades in woe, for they came of the fat southlands and the wide highways and the iron legions, and not of Killorn and its harsh windy loneliness.

Before long word came that the barbarian leaders were expected at the palace. So Bram, Nessa, and Kery put on their polished byrnies, and over them tunics and cloaks of their best plunder. They slung their swords over their shoulders and mounted their hests and rode between two squads of Ryvanian guardsmen through the gates and into the city.

It was packed and roiling with those who had fled. Crowds surged aimlessly around the broad avenues and spilled into the colonnaded temples and the looming apartments and even the gardens and villas of the nobility.

There was the dusty, bearded peasant, clinging to his

wife and his children and looking on the world with frightened eyes. Gaily decked noble, riding through the mob with patrician hauteur and fear underneath it. Fat merchant and shaven priest, glowering at the refugees who came in penniless to throng the city and must, by the queen's orders, be fed and housed. Patrolling soldiers, striving to keep order in the mindless whirlpool of man, their young faces drawn and their shoulders stooped beneath their mail. Jugglers, mountebanks, thieves, harlots, tavern-keepers, plying their trades in the feverish gaiety of doom; a human storm foaming off into strange half-glimpsed faces in darkened alleys and eddying crowds, the unaccountable aliens who flit through all great cities—the world seemed gathered at Ryvan, and huddling before the wrath that came.

Fear rode the city. Kery could feel it; he breathed and the air was dank with terror, he bristled animal-like and laid a hand to his sword. For an instant he remembered Killorn, the wide lake rose before him and he stood at its edge, watching the breeze ruffle it and hearing the whisper of reeds and the chuckle of water on a pebbled shore. Miles about lay the hills and the moors, the clean strong smell of ling was a drunkenness in his nostrils. It was silent save for the small cool wind that ruffled Morna's hair. And in the west it was sunset, the mighty sun-disc lay just below the horizon and a shifting, drifting riot of colors, flames of red and green and molten gold, burned in the twilit heavens.

He shook his head, feeling his longing as a sharp clear pain, and urged his hest through the crowds. Presently they reached the palace.

It was long and low and gracious, crowded now since all the nobles and their households had moved into it and, under protest, turned their own villas over to the homeless. Dismounting, the northerners walked between files of guardsmen, through fragrant gardens and up the broad marble steps of the building—through long corridors and richly furnished rooms, and finally into the audience chamber of Queen Sathi.

It was like a chalice of white stone, wrought in loveliness and brimming with twilight and stillness. That deep blue dusk, lay cool and mysterious between the high slim pillars, and somewhere came the rippling of a harp and the singing of birds and fountains. Kery felt suddenly aware of his uncouth garments and manners and accent. His tongue thickened and he did not know what to do with his hands. Awkwardly he took off his helmet.

"Lord Bram of Killorn, your majesty," said the chamberlain.

"Greeting, and welcome," said Sathi.

WORD had spread far about Ryvan's young queen but Kery thought dazedly that the gossips had spoken less of her than was truth. She was tall and lithe and sweetly formed, with strength slumbering deep under the wide soft mouth and the lovely curves of cheeks and forehead. Blood of the Sun Lands darkened her hair to a glowing blue-black and tinted her skin with gold, there was fire from the sun within her. Like other southern women, she dressed more boldly than the girls of Killorn, a sheer gown falling from waist to ankles, a thin veil over the shoulders, little jewelry. She needed no ornament.

She could not be very much older than he, if at all, thought Kery. He caught her great dark eyes on him and felt a slow hot flush go up his face. With an effort he checked himself and stood very straight, with his strange blue eyes like cold flames.

Beside Sathi sat the general, Jonan, and there were a couple of older men who seemed to be official advisors. But it soon was clear that only the queen and the soldier had much to say in this court.

Bram's voice boomed out, shattering the peace of the blue dusk for all his great size and ruddy beard he seemed lost in the ancient grace of the chamber. He spoke too loudly. He stood too stiff. "Thank you, my lady. But I am no lord, I simply head of this group of the men of Killorn." He waved clumsily at his fellows. "These are Nessa of Dagh and Kery of Broina."

"Be seated, then, and welcome again." Sathi's voice was low and musical. She signaled her servants to bring wine.

"We have heard of great wanderings in the north," she went on, when they had drunk. "But those lands are little known to us. What brought you so far from home?"

Nessa, who had the readiest tongue, answered. "There was famine in the land, your majesty. For three years drought and cold lay like iron aver Killorn. We hungered, and the coughing sickness came over many of us. Not all our magics and sacrifices availed to end our misery, they seemed only to raise great storms that destroyed what little we had kept.

"Then the weather smiled again, but as often happens, the gray blight came in the wake of the hard years. It reaped our grain before we could, the stalks withered and crumbled before our eyes, and wild beasts came in hunger-driven swarms to raid our dwindling flocks. There was scarce food enough for a quarter of our starving folk. We knew, from what had happened in other lands, that the gray blight will waste a country for years, five or ten, leaving only perhaps a third part of the crop alive at each harvest. Then it passes away and does not come again. But meanwhile the land will not bear many folk. s

"So in the end the clans decided that most must move away leaving only the few who could keep alive through the niggard years to hold the country for us. Hearts broke in twain, your majesty, for the hills and the moors and the lake where it is forever sunset were part of us. We are of that land and if we die away from it our ghosts will wander home. But go we must, lest all die."

"Yes, go on," said Jonan impatiently when he paused.

Bram gave him an angry look and took up the story. "Four hosts were to wander out of the land and see what would befall. If they found a place to stay they would abide there till the evil time was over. Otherwise they would live however they could. It lay with the gods, my lady, and we have traveled far from the realms of our gods.

"One host went eastward, into the great forests of Norla. One got ships and sailed west, out into the Day Lands where some of our adventurers had already explored a little way. One followed the coast southwestward, through country beyond our ken. And ours marched due south. And so we have wandered for five years."

"Homeless," whispered Sathi, and Kery thought her eyes grew bright with tears.

"Barbarian robbers!" snapped Jonan. "I know of the havoc they have wrought on their way."

"And what would you have done," growled Bram. Jonan gave him a stiff glare, but he rushed on. "Your majesty, we have taken only what we needed..."

And whatever else struck our fancy, thought Kery in a moment's wryness.

"—and much of our fighting has been done for honest pay. We want only a place to live a few years, land to farm as free yeomen, and we will defend the country, which shelters us, as long as we are in it. We are too few to take that land and hold it against a whole nation—that is why we have not settled down ere this—but on the march we will scatter my army in the world or leave our corpses for carrion birds. The men of Killorn keep faith with friends and foes alike, help to the one and harm to the other.

"Now we saw many fair fields in Ryvan where we could be at home. The Ganasthi have cleared off the owners for us. So we offer you this—give us the land we need and we will fight for you against these Ganasthi or any other foes while blood runs through our hearts. Refuse us and we may be able to make friends with the Dark Landers instead. For friends we must have."

"You see?" snarled Jonan. "He threatens banditry."

"No, no, you are too hasty," replied Sathi. "He is simply telling the honest truth. And the gods know we need warriors."

"This general was anxious enough for our help out there in the eastern marches," said Kery suddenly.

"Enough, barbarian," said Jonan with ice in his tones.

Color flared in Sathi's cheeks. "Enough of you, Jonan. These are brave and honest men, and our guests, and our sorely needed allies. We will draw up the treaty at once."

The general shrugged, insolently. Kery was puzzled. There was anger here, crackling under a hard-held surface, but it seemed new and strange. *Why?*

They haggled for a while over terms, Nessa doing most of the talking for Killorn. He and Bram would not agree that clansmen should owe fealty or even respect to any noble of Ryvan save the queen herself. Also they should have the right to go home whenever they heard the famine was over. Sathi was willing enough to concede it but Jonan had to be almost beaten down. Finally he gave grudging assent and the queen had her scribes draw the treaty up on parchment.

"That is not how we do it in Killorn," said Bram. "A tyr must be sacrificed and vows made on the ring of Llugan and the pipes of the gods."

Sathi smiled. "Very well, Red One," she nodded. "We will make the pledge thusly too, if you wish." With a sudden flame of bitterness, "What difference does it make? What difference does anything make now?"

CHAPTER FIVE

NOW the armies of Ganasth moved against Ryvan City itself. From all the plundered empire they streamed in, to ring the town in a living wall and hem the defenders within a fence of spears. And when the whole host was gathered, which took about ten sleeps from the time the Killorners arrived, they stormed the city.

Up the long slope of the hills on which Ryvan stood they came, running, bounding, holding up shields against the steady hail of missiles from the walls. Forward, silent and blank-faced, no noise in them save the crashing of thousands of feet and the high demon-music of their war-making—dying, strewing the ground with their corpses, but leaping over the fallen and raging against the walls.

Up ladders! Rams thundering at the gates! Men springing to the top of walls and toppling before the defenders and more of them snarling behind!

Back and forth the battle raged, now the Ryvanians driven back to the streets and rooftops, now the Dark Landers pressed to the edge of the walls and pitchforked over. Houses began to burn, here and there, and it was Sathi who made fire brigades out of those who could not fight. Kery had a glimpse of her from afar, as he battled on the outer parapets, a swift and golden loveliness against the leaping red.

After long and vicious fighting the northern gate went down. But Bram had foreseen this. He had pulled most of his barbarians thither, with Kery's bulls in their lead. He planted them well back and had a small stout troop on either side of the great buckling doors. When the barrier sagged on its hinges, the Ganasthi roared in unopposed, streaming through the entrance and down the broad bloody avenue.

Then the Killorners thrust from the side, pinching off the several hundred who had entered. They threw great jars of oil on the broken gates and set them ablaze, a barrier of flame which none could cross. And then Kery rode his bulls against the enemy, and behind him came the might of Killorn.

It was raw slaughter. Erelong they were hunting the foe up and down the streets and spearing them like wild animals. Meanwhile Bram got some engineers from Jonan's force who put up a temporary barricade in the now open gateway and stood guard over it.

The storm faded, grumbled away in surges of blood and whistling arrows. Shaken by their heavy losses, the Dark Landers pulled back out of missile range, ringed the city with their watchfires, and prepared to lay siege.

There was jubilation in Ryvan. Men shouted and beat their dented shields with nicked and blunted swords. They tossed their javelins in the air, emptied wineskins, and kissed the first and best girl who came to hand. Weary, bleeding, reft of many good comrades, and given at best a reprieve, the folk still snatched at what laughter remained.

Bram came striding to meet the queen. He was a huge and terrible figure stiff with dried blood, the ax blinking on his shoulder and the other hairy paw clamped on the neck of a tall Dark Lander whom he helped along with an occasional kick. Yet Sathi's dark eyes trailed to the slim form of Kery, following in the chief's wake and too exhausted to say much.

"I caught this fellow in the streets, my lady," said Bram merrily, "and since he seemed to be a leader I thought I'd better hang on to him for a while."

The invader stood motionless, regarding them with a chill yellow stare in which there lay an iron pride. He was tall and well built, his black mail silver-trimmed, a silver star on the battered black helmet. The snowy hair and beard stirred faintly in the breeze.

"An aristocrat, I would say," nodded Sathi. She herself seemed almost too tired to stand. She was smudged with smoke and her dress was torn and her small hands bleeding from their recent burdens. But she pulled herself erect and fought to speak steadily. "Yes, he may well be of value to us. That was good work. Aye, you men of Killorn fought nobly, without you we might well have lost the city. It was a good month when you came."

"It was no way to fight," snapped Jonan. He was tired and wounded himself, but there was no comradeship in the look he gave the northerners. "The risk of it—why, if you hadn't been able to seal the gate behind them, Ryvan would have fallen then and there."

"I did not see you doing much of anything when the gate was splintering before them," answered Bram curtly. "As it is, my lady, we've inflicted such heavy losses on them that I doubt they'll consider another attempt at storming. Which gives us at least time to try something else," He yawned mightily. "Time to sleep!"

JONAN stepped up close to the prisoner, and they exchanged a long look. There was no way to read the Dark Lander's thoughts but Kery thought he saw a tension under the general's hard-held features.

"I don't know what value a food-eating prisoner is to us

when he can't even speak our language," said the Ryvanian. "However, I can take him in charge if you wish."

"Do," she nodded dully.

"Odd if he couldn't talk any Aluardian at all," said Kery. "Wanderers through alien lands almost have to learn. The leaders of invading armies ought to know the tongue of their enemy, or at least have interpreters," He grinned with the cold savagery of the Broina. "Let the women of Killorn, the ones who've lost husbands today, have him for a while. I daresay he'll soon discover he knows your speech—whatever is left of him."

"No," said Jonan flatly. He signaled to a squad of his men. "Take this fellow down to the palace dungeons and give him something to eat. I'll be along later."

Kery started to protest but Sathi laid a hand on his arm. He felt how it was still bleeding a little and grew silent.

"Let Jonan take care of it," she said, her voice flat with weariness. "We all need rest now—O gods, to sleep!"

The Killorners had moved their wagons into the great forum and camped there, much to the disgust of the aristocrats and to the pleasure of whatever tavern keepers and unattached young women lived nearby. But Sathi had insisted that their three chiefs should be honored guests at the palace and it pleased them well enough to have private chambers and plenty of servants and the best of wine.

Kery woke in his bed and lay for a long while, drowsing and thinking the wanderous thoughts of half-asleep. When he got up he groaned, for he was stiff with his wounds and the long fury of battle. A slave came in and rubbed him with oil and brought him a barbarian-sized meal, after which he felt better.

But now he was restless. He felt the letdown that is the aftermath of high striving. It was hard to fight back the misery and loneliness that rose in him. He prowled the room unhappily, pacing under the glowing cressets, flinging himself on a couch and then springing to his feet again. The walls were a cage.

The city was a cage, a trap, he was caught like a snared beast and never again would he walk the moors of Killorn. Sharply as a knife thrust, he remembered hunting once out in the heath. He had gone alone, with spear and bow and a shaggy half-wild cynor loping at his heels, out after antlered prey somewhere beyond the little village. Long had they roamed, he and his beast, until were far from sight of man and only the great gray and purple and gold of the moors were around them.

The carpet under his bare feet seemed again to be the springy, pungent ling of Killorn. It was as if he smelled the sharp wild fragrance of it and felt the leaves brushing his ankles. It had been gray and windy, clouds rushed out of the west on a mounting gale. There was rain in the air and high overhead a single bird of prey had wheeled and looped on lonely wings. O almighty gods, how the wind had sung and cried to him, chilled his body with raw wet gusts and skirled in the dales and roared beneath the darkening heavens! And he had come down a long rocky slope into a wooded glen, a waterfall rushed and foamed along his path, white and green and angry black. He had sheltered in a mossy cave, lain and listened to the wind and the rain and the crystal, ringing waterfall, and when the weather cleared he had gotten up and gone home. There had been no quarry, but by Morna of Dagh, that failure meant more to him than all his victories since!

He picked up the pipe of the gods, where it lay with his armor, and turned it over and over in his hands. Old it was, dark with age, the pipes were of some nameless iron-like wood and the bag of a leather such as was never seen now. It was worn with the uncounted generations of Broinas who had had it, men made hard and stern by their frightful trust.

It had scattered the legions of the southerners who came conquering a hundred years ago and it had quelled the raiding savages from Norla and it had gone with one-eyed Alrigh and shouted down the walls of a city. And more than once, on this last dreadful march, it had saved the men of Killorn.

Now it was dead. The Piper of Killorn had fallen and the secret had perished with him and the folk it had warded were trapped like animals to die of hunger and pestilence in a strange land—*O Rhiach, Rhiach my father, come back from the dead, come back and put the pipe to your cold lips and play the war song of Killorn!*

Kery blew in it for the hundredth time and only a hollow whistling sounded in the belly of the instrument. Not even a decent tune, he thought bitterly.

He couldn't stay indoors, he had to get out under the sky again or go mad. Slinging the pipe over his shoulder he went out the door and up a long stairway to the palace roof gardens.

They slept all around him, sleep and silence were heavy in the long corridors. It was as if he were the last man alive and walked alone through the ruins of the world. He came out on the roof and went over to the parapet and stood looking out.

The moon was near the zenith, which meant, at this longitude, that it was somewhat less than half full and would dwindle as it sank westward. It rode serene in the dusky sky adding its pale glow to the diffused light, which filled all the Twilight Lands, and to the white pyre of the hidden sun. The city lay dark and silent under the sky, sleeping heavily, only the muted tramp of sentries and their ringing calls drifted up to Kery. Beyond the town burned the ominous red circle of the Ganasthi fires and he could see their tents and the black forms of their warriors.

They were settling down to a patient deathwatch. All the land had become silent waiting for Ryvan to die. It did not seem right that he should stand here among fragrant gardens and feel the warm western breeze on his face, not when steadfast Lluwynn and Baroda the Strong and gay young Kormak his comrade were ashen corpses with the women of Killorn keening over them—*O Killorn, Killorn, and the lake of sunset, have their ghosts gone home to you? Greet Morna for me, Kormak, whisper in the wind that I love her; tell her not to grieve.*

HE GREW aware that someone else was approaching, and turned with annoyance. But his mood lightened when he saw that it was Sathi. She was very fair as she walked toward him, young and lithe and beautiful, with the dark unbound hair floating about her.

"Are you up, Kery?" she asked, sitting down on the parapet beside him.

"Of course, my lady, or else you are dreaming," he smiled with a tired humor.

"Stupid question wasn't it?" She smiled back with a curving of closed lips that was lovely to behold. "But I am not feeling very bright just now."

"None of us are, my lady."

"Oh, forget that sort of address, Kery. I am too lonely as it is, sitting on a throne above all the world. Call me by my name, at least."

"You are very kind—Sathi."

"That is better." She smiled again, wistfully. "How you fought today! How you reaped them! What sort of a warrior are you, Kery, to ride wild bulls as if they were hests?"

"We of clan Broina have tricks. We feel things that other men do not seem to." Kery sat down beside her feeling the frozenness within him ease a little. "Aye, it can be lonely to wield power and you wonder if you are fit for it, not so? My father died in our first battle with the Ganasthi, and now I am the Broina, but who am I to lead my clan? I cannot even perform the first duty of my post."

"And what is that?" she asked.

He told her about the god-pipe. He showed it to her and gave her the tales of its singing. "You feel your flesh shiver and your bones begin to crumble, rocks dance and mountains groan and the gates of hell open before you but now the pipes are forever silent, Sathi. No man knows how to play them."

"I heard of your music at that battle," she nodded gravely, "and wondered why it was not sounded again this time," Awe and fear were in her eyes, the hand that touched the scarred sack trembled a little. "And this is the pipe of Killorn! You cannot play it again? You cannot find out how? It would be the saving of Ryvan and of your own folk and perhaps of all the Twilight Lands, Kery."

"I know, but what can I do? Who can understand the powers of heaven or unlock the doors of hell save Llugan Longsword himself?"

"I do not know. But Kery—I wonder. This pipe...do you really think that gods and not men wrought it?"

"Who but a god could make such a thing, Sathi?"

"I do not know, I say. And yet— Tell me, have you any idea of what the world is like in Killorn? Do you think it a flat plain with the sun hanging above, forever fixed in one spot?"

"Why I suppose so. Though we have met men in the southlands who claimed the world was a round ball and went about the sun in such a manner as always to turn the same face to it."

"Yes, the wise men of Ryvan tell us that that must be the case. They have learned it by studying the fixed stars and those that wander. Those others are worlds like our own, they say, and the fixed stars are suns a very long ways off. And we have a very dim legend of a time once, long and long and long ago, when this world did not eternally face the sun either. It spun like a top so that each side of it had light and dark alternately."

Kery knitted his brows trying to see that for himself. At last he nodded. "Well, it may have been. What of it?"

"The barbarians all think the world was born in flame and thunder many ages ago. But some of our thinkers believe that this creation was a catastrophe that destroyed that older world I speak of. There are dim legends and here and there we find very ancient ruins, cities greater than any we know today but buried and broken so long ago that even their building stones are almost weathered away. These thinkers believe that man grew mighty on this forgotten world which spun about itself, that his powers were like those we today call divine.

"Then something happened. We cannot imagine what, though a wise man once told me he believed all things attract each other—that is the reason why they fall to the ground he said—and that another world swept so close to ours that its pull stopped the spinning and yanked the moon closer than it had been."

Kery clenched his fists. "It could be," he murmured.

"It could well be, for what happens to an unskillful rider when his hest stops all at once? He goes flying over its head, right? Even so, this braking of the world would have brought earthquakes greater than we can imagine, quakes that leveled everything!"

"You have a quick wit. That is what this man told me. At any rate, only a very few people and animals lived and nothing remained of their great works save legends. In the course of many ages, man and beasts alike changed, the beasts more than man who can make his own surroundings to suit. Life spread from the Day Lands through the Twilight Zone. Plants got so they could use what little light we have here. Finally even the Dark Lands were invaded by the pallid growths which can live there. Animals followed and man came after the animals until today things are as you see."

She turned wide and serious eyes on him. "Could not this pipe have been made in the early days by a man who knew some few of the ancient secrets? No god but a man even as you, Kery. And what one man can make another can understand!"

HOPE rose in him and sagged again. "How?" he asked dully. And then, seeing the tears glimmer in her eyes: "Oh, it may all be true. I will try my best. But I do not even know where to begin."

"Try," she whispered. "Try!"

"But do not tell anyone that the pipe is silent, Sathi. Perhaps I should not even have told you."

"Why not? I am your friend and the friend of your folk, I would we had all the tribes of Killorn here."

"Jonan is not," he said grimly.

"Jonan—he is a harsh man, yes. But..."

"He does not like us, I do not know why but he doesn't."

"He is a strange one," she admitted. "He is not even of Ryvanian birth, he is from Guria, a city that we conquered long ago, though of course its people have long been full citizens of the empire. He wants to marry me, did you know?" She smiled. "I could not help laughing for he is so stiff. One would as soon wed an iron cuirass."

"Aye—wed—" Kery fell silent, and there was a dream in his gaze as he looked over the hills.

"What are you thinking of?" she asked after a while.

"Oh—home," he said. "I was wondering if I would ever see Killorn again."

She leaned over closer to him. One long black lock brushed his hand and he caught the faint fragrance of her. "Is it so fair a land?" she asked softly.

"No," he said. "It is harsh and gray and lonely. Storm winds sweep in and the sea roars on rocky beaches and men grow gnarled with wresting life from the stubborn soil. But there is space and sky and freedom, there are the little huts and the great halls, the chase and the games and the old songs around leaping fires, and…well…" His voice trailed off.

"You left a woman behind, didn't you?" she murmured gently.

He nodded. "Morna of Dagh, she of the sun-bright tresses and the fair young form and the laughter that was like rain showering on thirsty ground. We were very much in love."

"But she did not come too?"

"No. So many wanted to come that the unwed had to draw lots and she lost. Nor could I stay behind for I was heir to the Broina and the god-pipes would be mine someday." He laughed, a harsh sound like breaking iron. "You see how much good that has done me!"

"But even so—you could have married her before leaving?"

"No. Such hasty marriage is against clan law and Morna would not break it." Kery shrugged. "So we wandered out of the land, and I have not seen her since. But she will wait for me and I for her. We'll wait till—" He had half raised his hand but as he saw again the camp of the besiegers it fell helplessly to his lap.

"And you would not stay?" Sathi's tones were so low he had to bend his head close to hear. "Even if somehow Ryvan threw back its foes and valiant men were badly needed and could rise to the highest honors of the empire, you would not stay here?"

For a moment Kery sat motionless, wrapping himself about his innermost being. He had some knowledge of women. There had been enough of them along the dusty way, brief encounters and a fading memory.

His soul had room only for the bright image of one unforgotten girl. It was plain enough what this woman, who was young and beautiful and a queen, was saying and he would not ordinarily have hung back.

Especially when the folk of Killorn were still strangers in a camp of allies who did not trust them very far, when Killorn needed every friend it could find. And the Broina were an elvish clan who had never let overly many scruples hold them.

Only—only he liked Sathi—as a human being. She was brave and generous and wise and she was, really, so pitiably young. She had had so little chance to learn the hard truths of living in the loneliness of the Imperium and only a scoundrel would hurt her.

She sighed, ever so faintly, and moved back a little. Kery thought he saw her stiffening. One does not reject the offer of a queen.

"Sathi," he said, "for you, perhaps, even a man of Killorn might forget his home."

She half turned to him, hesitating, unsure of herself and him. He took her in his arms and kissed her.

"Kery, Kery, Kery—" she whispered, and her lips stole back toward his.

He felt rather than heard a footfall and turned with the animal alertness of the barbarian. Jonan stood watching them.

"Pardon me," said the general harshly. His countenance was strained. Then suddenly, "Your majesty! This savage mauling you…"

Sathi lifted a proud dark head. "This is the prince consort of Imperial Ryvan," she said haughtily. "Conduct yourself accordingly. You may go."

Jonan snarled and lifted an arm. Kery saw the armed men step from behind the tall flowering hedges and his sword came out with a rasp of steel.

"Guards!" screamed Sathi.

The men closed in, some with swords, others with pikeshafts. Kery's blade whistled against one shield, narrowly missing the man's horned helmet. Another came from each side. Sathi pulled her own blade. Pikeshafts thudded against Kery's bare head—

He fell, toppling into a roaring darkness while they clubbed him again. Down and down and down, whirling into a chasm of night. Dimly, just before blankness came, he saw the white beard and the mask-like face of the prince from Ganasth.

CHAPTER SIX

IT WAS a long and hard ride before they stopped and Kery almost fell from the hest to which they had bound him.

"I should have thought that you would soon awake," said the man from Ganasth. He had a soft voice and spoke Aluardian well enough. "I am sorry. It is no way to treat a man, carrying him like a sack of meal. Here…" He poured a glass of wine and handed it to the barbarian. "From now on you shall ride erect."

Kery gulped thirstily and felt a measure of strength flowing back. He looked around him.

They had gone steadily eastward and were now camped near a ruined farmhouse. A fire was crackling and one of the score or so of enemy warriors was roasting a haunch of meat over it. The rest stood leaning on their weapons and their cold amber eyes never left the two prisoners.

Sathi stood near bleak-faced Jonan and her great dark eyes never left Kery. He smiled at her shakily and with a little sob she took a step toward him. Jonan pulled her back roughly.

"Kery," she whispered. "Kery, are you well?"

"As well as could be expected," he said wryly. Then to the Ganasthian prince, "What is this, anyway? I woke up to find myself joggling eastward and that is all I know. What is your purpose?"

"We have several," answered the alien. He sat down near the fire pulling his cloak around him against the chill that blew out of the glooming east. His impassive face watched the dance of flames as if they told him something.

Kery sat down as well, stretching his long legs easily. He might as well relax he thought. They had taken his sword and his pipes and they were watching him like hungry beasts. There was never a chance to fight.

"Come, Sathi," he waved to the girl. "Come over here by me."

"No!" snapped Jonan.

"Yes, if she wants to," said the Ganasthian mildly.

"By that filthy barbarian…"

"None of us have washed recently," The gentle tones were suddenly like steel. "Do not forget, General, that I am Mongku of Ganasth and heir apparent to the throne."

"And I rescued you from the city," snapped the man. "If it weren't for me you might well be dead at the hands of that red savage."

"That will do," said Mongku. "Come over here and sit by us, Sathi."

His guardsmen stirred, unacquainted with the Ryvanian tongue but sensing the clash of wills. Jonan shrugged sullenly and stalked over to sit opposite them. Sathi fled to Kery and huddled against him. He comforted her awkwardly. Over her shoulder he directed a questioning look at Mongku.

"I suppose you deserve some explanation," said the Dark Lander. "Certainly Sathi must know the facts," He leaned back on one elbow and began to speak in an almost dreamy tone.

"When Ryvan conquered Guria, many generations ago, some of its leaders were proscribed. They fled eastward and so eventually wandered into the Dark Lands and came to Ganasth. It was then merely a barbarian town but the

Gurians became advisors to the king and began teaching the people all the arts of civilization. It was their hope one day to lead the hosts of Ganasth against Ryvan, partly for revenge and partly for the wealth and easier living to be found in the Twilight Lands. Life is hard and bitter in the eternal night, Sathi. It is ever a struggle merely to keep alive. Can you wonder so very much that we are spilling into your gentler climate and your richer soil?

"Descendants of the Gurians have remained aristocrats in Ganasth. But Jonan's father conceived the idea of moving back with a few of his friends to work from within against the day of conquest. At that time we were bringing our neighbors under our heel and looked already to the time when we should move against the Twilight Lands. At any rate he did this and nobody suspected that he was aught but a newcomer from another part of Ryvan's empire. His son, Jonan, entered the army and, being shrewd and strong and able, finally reached the high post that you yourself bestowed on him, Sathi."

"Oh, no—Jonan—" She shuddered against Kery.

"Naturally when we invaded at last he had to fight against us, and for fear of prisoners revealing his purpose very few Ganasthians know who he really is. A risk was involved, yes. But it is convenient to have a general of the enemy on your side! Jonan is one of the major reasons for our success.

"Now we come to myself, a story which is very simply told, I was captured and it was Jonan's duty as a citizen of Ganasth to rescue his prince—quite apart from the fact that I do know his identity and torture might have loosened my tongue. He might have effected my escape easily enough without attracting notice, but other factors intervened. For one thing, there was this barbarian alliance, and especially that very dangerous new weapon they had which he had observed in use. We clearly could not risk its being turned on us. Indeed we almost had to capture it. Then, too, Jonan is desirous of marrying you, Sathi, and I must say that it seems a good idea. With you as a hostage Ryvan, will be more amenable. Later you can return as nominal ruler of your city, a vassal of Ganasth, and that will make our conquest easier to administer. Though not too easy, I fear. The Twilight Landers will not much like being transported into the Dark Lands to make room for us."

Sathi began to cry, softly and hopelessly. Kery stroked her hair and said nothing.

Mongku sat up and reached for the chunk of meat his soldier handed him. "So Jonan and his few trusty men let me out of prison and we went up to the palace roof after you, who had been seen going that way shortly before. Listening a little while to your conversation we saw that we had had the good luck to get that hell-pipe of the north, too. So we took you. Jonan was for killing you, Kery my friend, but I pointed out that you could be useful in many ways such as a means for making Sathi listen to reason. Threats against you will move her more than against herself, I think."

"You crawling louse," said Kery tonelessly.

Mongku shrugged. "I'm not such a bad sort, but war is war and I have seen the folk of Ganasth hungering too long to have much sympathy for a bunch of fat Twilight Landers.

"At any rate, we slipped out of the city unobserved. Jonan could not remain, for when the queen and I were both missing, and he responsible for both, it would be plain to many whom to accuse. Moreover, Sathi's future husband is too valuable to lose in a fight. And I myself would like to report to my father the king as to how well the war has gone.

"So we are bound for Ganasth."

There was a long silence while the fire leaped and crackled and the stars blinked far overhead. Finally Sathi shook herself and sat erect and said in a small hard voice, "Jonan, I swear you will die if you wed me, I promise you that."

The officer did not reply. He sat brooding into the dusk with a look of frozen contempt and weariness on his face.

Sathi huddled back against Kery's side and soon she slept.

ON AND on. They were out of the Twilight Lands altogether now. Night had fallen on them and still they rode eastward. They were tough, these Ganasthi, they stopped only for sleep and quickly gulped food and a change of mounts and the miles reeled away behind them.

Little was said on the trail. They were too tired at the halts and seemingly in too much of a hurry while riding. With Sathi there could only be a brief exchange of looks, a squeeze of hands, and a few whispered words with the glowing-eyed men of Ganasth looking on. She was a gallant girl, thought Kery. The cruel trek told heavily on her but she rode without complaint—she was still queen of Ryvan!

Ryvan, Ryvan, how long could it hold out now in the despair of its loss? Kery thought that Red Bram might be able to seize the mastery and whip the city into fighting pitch but warfare by starvation was not to the barbarians' stomachs. They could not endure a long siege.

But what lay ahead for him and her and the captured

weapon of the gods?

Never had he been in so grim a country. It was dark, eternally dark, night and cold and the brilliant frosty stars lay over the land, shadows and snow and a whining wind that ate and ate and gnawed its way through furs and flesh down to the bone. The moon got fuller here than it ever did over the Twilight Belt, its chill white radiance spilled on reaching snowfields and glittered like a million pinpoint stars fallen frozen to earth.

He saw icy plains and tumbled black chasms and fanged crags sheathed in glaciers. The ground rang with cold. Cramped and shuddering in his sleeping bag, he heard the thunder of frost-split rocks, the sullen boom and rumble of avalanches, now and again the faint far despairing howl of prowling wild beasts of prey.

"How can anyone live here?" he asked Mongku once. "The land is dead. It froze to death ten thousand years ago."

"It is a little warmer in the region of Ganasth," said the prince. "Volcanoes and hot springs. And there is a great sea that has never frozen over. It has fish, and animals that live off them, and men that live off the animals. But in truth only the broken and hunted of man can ever have come here. We are the disinherited and we are claiming no more than our rightful share of life in returning to the Twilight Lands."

He added thoughtfully; "I have been looking at that weapon of yours, Kery. I think I know the principle of its working. Sound does many strange things and there are even sounds too low or too high for the human ear to catch. A singer who holds the right note long enough can make a wine glass vibrate in sympathy until it shatters. We built a bridge once, over Thunder Gorge near Ganasth, but the wind blowing between the rock walls seemed to make it shake in a certain rhythm that finally broke it. Oh, yes, if the proper sympathetic notes can be found, much may be done.

"I don't know what hell's music that pipe is supposed to sound, but I found that the reeds can be tautened or loosened and that the shape of the bag can be subtly altered by holding it in the right way. Find the proper combination and I can well believe that even the small noise made with one man's breath can kill and break and crumble."

He nodded his gaunt half-human face in the ruddy blaze of fire. "Aye, I'll find the notes, Kery, and then the pipe will play for Ganasth."

The barbarian shuddered with more than the cold, searching wind. Gods, gods, if he did—if the pipes should sound the final dirge of Killorn!

FOR a moment he had a wild desire to fling himself on Mongku, rip out the prince's throat and kill the score of enemy soldiers with his hands. But no—no—it wouldn't do. He would die before he had well started and Sathi would be alone in the Dark Lands.

He looked at her, sitting very quiet near the tire. The wavering light seemed to wash her fair young form in blood. She gave him a tired and hopeless smile.

Brave girl, brave girl, wife for a warrior in all truth. But there was the pipe and there was Killorn and there was Morna waiting for him to come home.

They were nearing Ganasth, he knew. They had ridden past springs that seethed and bubbled in the snow, seen the red glare of volcanoes on the jagged horizon, passed fields of white fungus-growths that the Dark Landers cultivated.

Soon the iron gates would clash shut on him and what hope would there be then?

He lay back in his sleeping bag trying to think. He had to escape. Somehow he must escape with the pipe of the gods. But if he tried and went down with a dozen spears in him there was an end of all hope.

The wind blew, drifting snow across the sleepers. Two men stood guard and their strangely glowing eyes never left the captives. They could see in this realm of shadows where he was half-blind. They could hunt him down like an animal.

What to do? What to do?

On the road he went with his hands tied behind him, his ankles lashed to the stirrups, and his nest's bridle tied to the pommel of another man's saddle. No chance of escape there. But one must get up after sleep.

He rolled close to Sathi's quiet form as if he were merely turning over in slumber. His lips brushed against the leather bag and he wished it were her face.

"Sathi," he whispered as quietly as he could. "Sathi, don't move, but listen to me."

"Aye," her voice drifted back under the wind and the cold. "Aye, darling."

"I am going to make a break for it when we get up. Help me if you can but don't risk getting hurt. I don't think we can both get away but wait for me in Ganasth!"

She lay silent for a long while. Then she said, "As you will, Kery. And whatever comes, I love you."

He should have replied but the words stuck in his throat. He rolled back and, quite simply, went to sleep.

A spear butt prodding his side awoke him. He yawned mightily and sat up, loosening his bag around him, tensing every muscle in his body.

"The end of this ride will see us in the city," Mongku said.

Kery rose slowly, gauging distances. A guardsman stood beside him, spear loose in one hand. The rest were scattered around the camp or huddled close to the fire. The hests were a darker shadow bunched on the fringes.

Kery wrenched the spear of the nearest man loose, swinging one booted foot into his belly. He brought the weapon around in a smashing arc, cracking the heavy butt into another's jaw and rammed the head into the throat of a third. Even as he stabbed he was plunging into motion.

A Ganasthian yelled and thrust at him. Sathi threw herself on the shaft, pulling it down. Kery leaped for the hests.

There were two men on guard there. One drew a sword and hewed at the northerner. The keen blade slashed through heavy tunic and undergarments, cutting his shoulder—but not too badly. He came under the fellow's guard and smashed a fist into his jaw. Seizing the weapon he whirled and hacked at the other Dark Lander beating down the soldier's ax and cutting him across the face.

The rest of the camp was charging at him. Kery bent and cut the hobbles of the hest beside him. A shower of flung spears rained about him as he sprang to the saddleless back. Twisting his left hand into the long mane he kicked the frightened beast in the flanks and plunged free.

Two Ganasthi quartered across his trail. He bent low over the hest's back, spurring the mount with the point of his sword. As he rode down on them he hewed at one and saw him fall with a scream. The other stumbled out of the path of his reckless charge.

"Hai-ah!" shouted Kery.

He clattered away over the stony icy fields toward the shelter of the dark hills looming to the north. Spears and arrows whistled on his trail and he heard, dimly, the shouts of men and the thud of pursuing hoofs.

He was alone in a land of foes, a land of freezing cold where he could scarce see half a mile before him, a land of hunger and swords. They were after him and it would take all the hunter's skill he had learned in Killorn and all the warrior's craftiness taught by the march to evade them. And after that—Ganasth!

CHAPTER SEVEN

THE city loomed dark before him reaching with stony fingers for the ever-glittering stars. Of black stone it was, mountainous walls ringing in the narrow streets and the high gaunt houses. A city of night, city of darkness. Kery shivered.

Behind the city rose a mountain, a deeper shadow against the frosty dark of heaven. It was a volcano and from its mouth a red flame flapped in the keening wind. Sparks and smoke streamed over Ganasth. There was a hot smell of sulfur in the bitter air. The fire added a faint blood-like tinge to the cold glitter of moonlight and starlight on the snowfields.

There was a highway leading through the great main gates and the glowing-eyed people of the Dark Lands were trafficking along it. Kery strode directly on his way, through the crowds and ever closer to the city.

He wore the ordinary fur and leather dress of the country that he had stolen from an outlying house. The parka hood was drawn low to shadow his alien features. He went armed, as most men did, sword belted to his waist, and because he went quietly and steadily nobody paid any attention to him.

But if he were discovered and the hue and cry went up that would be the end of his quest.

A dozen sleeps of running and hiding in the wild hills, shivering with cold and hunger, hunting animals which could see where he was blind, and ever the men of

Ganasth on his trail—it would all go for naught. He would die and Sathi would be bound to a hateful pledge and Killorn would in time be the home of strangers.

He must finally have shaken off pursuit, he thought. Ranging through the hills he had found no sign of the warriors who had scoured them before. So he had proceeded toward the city on his wild and hopeless mission.

To find a woman and a weapon in the innermost citadel of a foe whose language even was unknown to him—truly the gods must be laughing!

He was close to the gates now. They loomed over him like giants, and the passage through the city wall was a tunnel. Soldiers stood on guard and Kery lowered his head.

Traffic streamed through. No one gave him any heed. But it was black as hell in the tunnel and only a Ganasthian could find his way. Blindly Kery walked ahead, bumping into people, praying that none of the angry glances he got would unmask his pretense.

When he came out into the street the breath was sobbing in his lungs. He pushed on down its shadowy length feeling the wind that howled between the buildings cold on his cheeks.

But where to go now, where to go?

Blindly he struck out toward the heart of town. Most rulers preferred to live at the center.

The Ganasthi were a silent folk. Men stole past in the gloom, noiseless save for the thin snow scrunching under their feet. Crowds eddied dumbly through the great market squares, buying and selling with a gesture or a whispered syllable. A city of half-seen ghosts. Kery felt more than half a ghost himself, shade of a madman flitting hopelessly to the citadel of the king of hell.

He found the place at last, more by blind blundering through the narrow twisting streets than anything else. Drawing himself into the shadow of a building across the way he stood looking at it, weighing his chances.

There was a high wall around the palace. He could only see its roof but it seemed to be set well back. He spied a gate not too far off, apparently a secondary entrance for it was small and only one sentry guarded it.

Now! By all the gods, now!

For a moment his courage failed him, and he stood sweating and shivering and licking dry lips. It wasn't fear of death. He had lived too long with the dark gods as comrade—he had but little hope of escaping alive from these nighted hills. But he thought of the task before him, and the immensity of it and the ruin that lay in his failure, and his heartbeat nearly broke through his ribs.

What, after all, could he hope to do? What was his plan, anyway? He had come to Ganasth on a wild and hopeless journey, scarcely thinking one sleep ahead of his death-dogged passage. Only now—now he must reach a decision, and he couldn't.

With a snarl, Kery started across the street.

NO ONE else was in sight, there was little traffic in this part of town, but at any moment someone might round either of the corners about which the way twisted and see what he was doing. He had to be fast.

He walked up to the sentry who gave him a haughty glance. There was little suspicion in it for what had anyone to fear in the hearth of Ganasth the mighty?

Kery drew his sword and lunged.

The sentry yelled and brought down his pike. Kery

batted the shaft aside even as he went by it. His sword flashed, stabbing for the other man's throat. With a dreadful gurgling the guard stumbled and went clattering to earth.

Now quickly!

Kery took the man's helmet and put it on. His own long locks were fair enough to pass for Ganasthian at a casual glance, and the visor would hide his eyes. Shedding his parka he slipped on the bloodstained tunic and the cloak over that. Taking the pike in hand he went through the gate.

Someone cried out and feet clattered in the street and along the garden paths before him. The noise had been heard. Kery looked wildly around at the pale bushes of fungus that grew here under the moon. He crawled between the fleshy fronds of the nearest big one and crouched behind it.

Guardsmen ran down the path. The moonlight blinked like cold silver on their spearheads. Kery wriggled on his stomach through the garden of fungus, away from the trail but toward the black palace.

Lying under a growth at the edge of a frost-silvered expanse of open ground he scouted the place he must next attack. The building was long and rambling, seemingly four stories high, built of polished black marble. There were two guards in sight, standing warily near a door. The rest must have run off to investigate the alarm.

Two—

Kery rose, catching his stride even as he did, and dashed from the garden toward them. The familiar helmet and tunic might assure them for the instant he needed but he had to run lest they notice.

"Vashtung!" shouted one of the men.

His meaning was plain enough. Kery launched his pike at the other, who still looked a bit uncertain. It was an awkward throwing weapon. It brought him down wounded in a clatter of metal. The other roared and stepped forth to meet the assault.

Kery's sword was out and whirring. He chopped at the pikeshaft that jabbed at him, caught his blade in the tough wood and pushed the weapon aside. As he came up face to face he kneed the Ganasthian with savage precision.

The other man reached up and grabbed his ankle and pulled him down. Kery snarled, the rage of battle rising in him. It was as if the pipes of Broina skirled in his head. Fear and indecision were gone. He got his hands on the soldier's neck and wrenched. Even as the spine snapped he was rising again to his feet.

He picked up sword and pike and ran up the stairs and through the door. Now Sathi! He had one ally in this house of hell.

A long and silent corridor, lit by dim red cressets, stretched before him. He raced down it and his boots woke hollow echoes that paced him through its black length.

Two men in the dress of servants stood in the room into which he burst. They stared wildly at him. He stabbed one but the other fled screaming. He'd give the alarm but there was no time to chase. No time!

A staircase wound up toward the second story and Kery took it, flying up three steps at a time. Dimly, below him, he heard the frantic tattoo of a giant gong, the alarm signal, but the demon fury was fire and ice in his blood.

Another servant gaped at him. Kery seized him with a rough hand and held the sword at his throat.

"Sathi," he snarled. "Sathi—Ryvan—Sathi!"

The Ganasthian gibbered in a panic that seemed weird with his frozen face. Kery grinned viciously and pinked him with the blade. "Sathi!" he said urgently, "Sathi of Ryvan!"

Shaking, the servant led the way, Kery urging him ungently to greater speed. They went up another flight of stairs and down a hallway richly hung with furs and tapestries. Passing lackeys gaped at them and some ran. Gods, they'd bring all Ganasth down on his neck!

Before a closed door stood a guardsman. Kery slugged the servant when he pointed at that entrance and ran to meet this next barrier. The guard yelled and threw up his pike.

Kery's own long-shafted weapon clashed forth. They stabbed at each other, seeking the vitals. The guardsman had a cuirass and Kery's point grazed off the metal. He took a ripping slash in his left arm. The Ganasthian bored in, wielding his pike with skill, beating aside Kery's guard.

CHAPTER EIGHT

THE Twilight Lander dropped his own weapon, seized the other haft in both hands, and wrenched. Grimly the Ganasthian hung on. Kery worked his way in closer. Suddenly he released the shaft, almost fell against his enemy, and drew the Dark Lander's sword. The short blade flashed and the sentry fell.

The door was barred. He beat on it frantically, hearing the clatter of feet coming up the stairs, knowing that a thunderstorm of hurled weapons was on its way. "Sathi!" he cried. "Sathi, it is Kery, let me in!"

The first soldiers appeared down at the end of the corridor. Kery threw himself against the door. It opened, and he plunged through and slammed down the bolt.

Sathi stood there and wonder was in her eyes. "Oh, Kery," she breathed, "Kery, you came…"

"No time," he rasped. "Where is the pipe of Killorn?"

She fought for calmness. "Mongku has it," she said. "His chambers are on the next floor, above these—"

The door banged and groaned as men threw their weight against it.

Sathi took his hand and led him into the next room. A fire burned low in the hearth. "I thought it out, against the time you might come," she said. "The only way out is up that chimney. It should take us to the roof and thence we can go down again."

"Oh, well done, lass!" With a sweep of the poker Kery scattered the logs and coals out on the carpet while Sathi barred the door into the next room. Drawing a deep breath the Killorner went into the fireplace, braced feet and back against the sides of the flue and began to climb up.

Smoke swirled in the chimney. He gasped for breath and his lungs seemed on fire. Night in here, utter dark and choking of fouled air. His heart roared and his strength ebbed from him. Up and up and up, hitch yourself still further up.

"Kery." Her voice came low, broken with coughing. "Kery—I can't. I'm slipping—"

"Hang on!" he gasped. "Here. Reach up. My belt—"

He felt the dragging weight catch at him, there in the smoke-thickened dark, and drew a grim breath and edged himself further, up and up and up.

And out!

He crawled from the chimney and fell to the roof with the world reeling about him and a rushing of darkness in his head. His tormented lungs sucked the bitter air. He sobbed and the tears washed the soot from his eyes. He stood up and helped Sathi to her feet.

She leaned against him, shuddering with strain and with the wind that cried up here under the flickering stars. He looked about, seeking a way down again. Yes, over there, a doorway opening on a small terrace. Quickly now.

They crawled over the slanting, ice-slippery roof, helping each other where they could, fighting a way to the battlement until Kery's grasping fingers closed on its edge and he heaved both of them up onto it.

"Come on!" he snapped. "They'll be behind us any moment now."

"What to do?" she murmured. "What to do?"

"Get the pipes!" he growled, and the demon blood of

Broina began to boil in him again. "Get the pipes and destroy them if we can do nothing else."

They went through the door and down a narrow staircase and came to the fourth floor of the palace.

Sathi looked up and down the long empty hallway. "I have been up here before," she said with a coolness that was good to hear. "Let me see—yes, this way, I think—" As they trotted down the hollow length of corridor she said further: "They treated me fairly well here, indeed with honor though I was a prisoner. But oh, Kery, it was like sunlight to see you again!"

He stooped and kissed her, briefly, wondering if he would ever have a chance to do it properly. Most likely not, but she would be a good companion on hell-road.

They came into a great antechamber. Kery had his sword out, the only weapon left to him, but no one was in sight. All the royal guards must be out hunting him. He grinned wolfishly and stepped to the farther door.

"Kery—" Sathi huddled close against him. "Kery, do we dare? It may be death—"

"It will be like that anyway," he said curtly and swung the door open.

A GREAT, richly furnished suite of chambers, dark and still, lay before him. He padded through the first, looking right and left like a questing animal, and into the next.

Two men stood there, talking—Jonan and Mongku.

They saw him and froze, for he was a terrible sight, bloody, black with smoke, fury cold and bitter blue in his eyes. He grinned, a white flash of teeth in his sooted face, and drew his sword and stalked forward.

"So you have come," said Mongku quietly.

"Aye," said Kery. "Where is the pipe of Killorn?"

Jonan thrust forward, drawing the sword at his belt. "I will hold him, prince," he said. "I will carve him into very bits for you."

Kery met his advance in a clash of steel. They circled, stiff-legged and wary, looking for an opening. There was death here. Sathi knew starkly that only one of those two would leave this room.

Jonan lunged in, stabbing, and Kery skipped back. The officer was better in handling these short swords than he who was used to the longer blades of the north. He brought his own weapon down sharply, deflecting the thrust. Jonan parried, and then it was bang and crash, thrust and leap and hack with steel clamoring and sparking. The glaives hissed and screamed, the fighters breathed hoarsely and there was murder in their eyes.

Jonan ripped off his cloak with his free hand and flapped it in Kery's face. The northerner hacked out, blinded, and Jonan whipped the cloth around to tangle his blade. Then he rushed in, stabbing. Kery fell to one knee and took the thrust on his helmet, letting it glide off. Reaching up he got Jonan around the waist and pulled the man down on him.

They rolled over, growling and biting and gouging. Jonan clung to his sword and Kery to that wrist. They crashed into a wall and struggled there.

Kery got one leg around Jonan's waist and pulled himself up on the man's chest. He got a two-handed grasp on the enemy's sword arm, slipped the crook of one elbow around, and broke the bone.

Jonan screamed. Kery reached over. He took the sword from his loosening fingers and buried it in Jonan's breast.

He stood up then, trembling with fury, and looked at

the pipes of Killorn.

It was almost as if Mongku's expressionless face smiled. The Ganasthian held the weapon cradled in his arms, the mouthpiece near his lips. He nodded. "I got it to working," he said. "In truth it is a terrible thing. Who holds it might well hold the world someday."

Kery stood waiting, the sword hanging limp in one hand.

"Yes," said Mongku. "I am going to play it."

Kery started across the floor—and Mongku blew.

THE sound roared forth, wild, cruel, seizing him and shaking him, ripping at nerve and sinew. Bone danced in his skull and night shouted in his brain. He fell to the ground, feeling the horrible jerking of his muscles, seeing the world swim and blur before him.

The pipes screamed. Goodnight, Kery, goodnight, goodnight! It is the dirge of the world he is playing, the coronach of Killorn, it is the end of all things skirling in your body—

Sathi crept forth. She was behind the player, the hell-tune did not strike her so deeply, but even as his senses blurred toward death Kery saw how she fought for every step, how the bronze lamp almost fell from her hand. Mongku had forgotten her. He was playing doom, watching Kery die and noting how the music worked.

Sathi struck him from behind. He fell, dropping the pipes, and turned dazed eyes up to her. She struck him again and again.

Then she hurried over to Kery and cradled his head in her arms and sobbed with the horror of it and with the need for haste. "Oh, quickly, quickly, beloved, we have to flee, they will be here now—I hear them in the hallway, come—"

Kery sat up. His head was ringing and thumping, his muscles burned and weakness was like an iron hand on him. But there was that which had to be done and it gave him strength from some forgotten wellspring. He rose on shaky legs and went over and picked up the bagpipe of the gods.

"No," he said.

"Kery…"

"We will not flee," he said. "I have a song to play."

She saw the cold remote mask of his face. He was not Kery now of the ready laugh and the reckless bravery and the wistful memories of a lost homestead. He had become something else with the pipe in his hands, something that stood stern and somber and apart from man. There seemed to be ghosts in the vast shadowy room, the blood of his fathers who had been Pipers of Killorn, and he was the guardian now. She shrank against him for protection. There was a small charmed circle that the music did not enter, but it was a stranger she stood beside.

Carefully Kery lifted the mouthpiece to his lips and blew. He felt the vibration tremble under his feet. The walls wavered before his eyes as unheard notes shivered the air. He himself heard no more than the barbarian screaming of the war music he had always known but he saw death riding out.

A troop of guardsmen burst through the door—halted, stared at the tall piper, and then howled in terror and pain.

Kery played. And as he played Killorn rose before him. He saw the reach of gray windswept moors, light glimmering on high cold tarns, birds winging in a sky of riven clouds. Space and loneliness and freedom, a hard open land of stern and bitter beauty, the rocks which had shaped his bones and the soil which had nourished his flesh. He stood by the great lake of sunset, storms swept in over it, rain and lightning, the waves dashed themselves to angry death on a beach of grinding stones.

He strode forward, playing, and the soldiers of Ganasth died before him. The walls of the palace trembled, hangings fell to the shuddering floor, the building groaned as the demon music sought and found resonance.

He played them a song of the chase, the long wild hunt over the heath, breath gasping in hot lungs and blood shouting in the ears, running drunk with wind after the prey that fled and soared. He played them fire and comradeship and the little huts crouched low under the mighty sky. And the walls cracked around him. Pillars trembled and broke. The roof began to cave in and everywhere they died about him.

He played war, the skirl of pipes and the shout of men, clamor of metal, tramp of feet and hoofs, and the fierce blink of light on weapons. He sang them up an army that rode over the rim of the world with swords aflame and arrows like rain and the whole building tumbled to rubble even as he walked out of it.

Tenderly, dreamily, he played of Morna the fair. Morna who had stood with him on the edge of the lake where it is forever sunset, listening to the chuckle of small wavelets and looking west to the pyre of red and gold and dusky purple, the eyes and the lips and the hair of Morna and what she and he had whispered to each other on that quiet shore. But there was death in that song.

The ground began to shake under Ganasth. There is but little strength in the lungs of one man and yet when that strikes just the right notes, and those small pushes touch off something else far down in the depths of the earth, the world will tremble. The Dark Landers rioted in a more than human fear, in the blind panic that the pipes sang to them.

The gates were closed before him, but Kery played them down. Then he turned and faced the city and played it a song of the wrath of the gods. He played them up rain and cold and scouring wind, glaciers marching from the north in a blind whirl of snow, lightning aflame in the heavens and cities ground to dust. He played them a world gone crazy, sundering continents and tidal waves marching over the shores and mountains flaming into a sky of rain and fire. He played them whirlwinds and dust storms and the relentless sleety blast from the north. He sang them ruin and death and the sun burning out to darkness.

When he ceased, and he and Sathi left the half-shattered city, none stirred to follow. None dared who were still alive. Outside the city Sathi fainted from exhaustion. Kery lifted her limp form as the snow swirled through the air. He thought he could see death in the winds that whipped around them. But when Sathi soon revived he knew they would survive the perilous trip back into the world of light. They must. It seemed to the two of them, as they struck out over the snowy plains, that the volcano behind was beginning to grumble and throw its flames a little higher.

CHAPTER NINE

HE STOOD alone in the gardens of Ryvan's palace looking out over the city. Perhaps he thought of the hard journey back from the Dark Lands. Perhaps he thought of the triumphant day when they had sneaked back into the fastness and then gone out again, the Piper of Killorn and Red Bram roaring in his wake to smash the siege and scatter the armies of Ganasth and send the broken remnants fleeing homeward. Perhaps he thought of the future—who knew? Sathi approached him quietly, wondering what to say.

He turned and smiled at her, the old merry smile she knew but with something else behind it. He had been the war god of Killorn and that left its mark on a man.

"So it all turned out well," he said.

"Thanks to you, Kery," she answered, softly.

"Oh, not so well at that," he decided. "There were too many good men who fell, too much laid waste. It will take a hundred years before all this misery is forgotten."

"But we reached what we strove for," she said. "Ryvan is safe, all the Twilight Lands are. You folk of Killorn have the land you needed. Isn't that enough to achieve?"

"I suppose so." Kery stirred restlessly. "I wonder how it stands in Killorn now?"

"And you still want to return?" She tried to hold back the tears. "This is a fair land, and you are great in it, all you people from the north. You would go back to—that?"

"Indeed," he said. "All you say is true. We would be fools to return," He scowled. "It may well be that in the time we yet have to wait most of us will find life better here and decide to stay. But not I, Sathi. I am just that kind of fool."

"This land needs you, Kery. I do."

He tilted her chin, smiling half sorrowfully into her eyes. "Best you forget, dear," he said. "I will not stay here once the chance comes to return."

She shook her head blindly, drew a deep breath, and said with a catch in her voice. "Then stay as long as you can, Kery."

"Do you really mean that?" he asked slowly.

She nodded.

"You are a fool too," he said. "But a very lovely fool."

He took her in his arms.

Presently she laughed a little and said, not without hope, "I'll have a while to change your mind, Kery. And I'll try to do it, I'll try!"

THE END

If you've enjoyed this book, you will not want to miss these terrific titles…

ARMCHAIR SCI-FI & HORROR DOUBLE NOVELS, $12.95 each

ARMCHAIR SCIENCE FICTION & FANTASY CLASSICS, $12.95 each

If you've enjoyed this book, you will not want to miss these terrific titles…

ARMCHAIR SCI-FI & HORROR DOUBLE NOVELS, $12.95 each

ARMCHAIR SCIENCE FICTION CLASSICS, $12.95 each

ARMCHAIR SCIENCE FICTION & HORROR GEMS SERIES, $12.95 each

BLUE GHOSTS FROM OUTER SPACE!

What was the undead secret of this awful world of ghosts—ghosts with the power to switch men's souls? The name of the planet was Amanas, and it had wondered through deep space for centuries. Underneath its ghostly-white layer of clouds were the remains of an ancient civilization. A civilization whose beings seemed to live forever—the Ilanu, great winged beings whose origins traced back to ancient Earth.

But there was also something else on this planet, something more terrifying than any sane man could ever imagine. But a mad, vengeance-seeking outcast from Earth conceived of harnessing the power of this strange horror—a power to be unleashed upon the unsuspecting citizens of Earth.

CAST OF CHARACTERS

DR. KIMBALL CRANE
He was trying to warn the Earth of an impending peril from outer space. Unfortunately no one seemed to be listening

PETER HAYMES
A brilliant scientist who was literally laughed off the Earth. He disappeared into deep space and was presumed dead.

JUDD RAFFERTY
He knew he wasn't supposed to report non-registry messages from deep space, but this one seemed too important to ignore.

STEVE
Marooned on a distant planet, he discovered the only way to survive was in something very simple—and very green!

TOMMY
The llanu thought he was a nottar, a simple hunter of the boranny. But strength and courage made him far more than that.

COMMANDER SCOTT
He was one of the few men in Military Intelligence who knew the real peril that threatened Earth from beyond the solar system.

CAPTAIN ANDREWS
He was ordered to a specific rendezvous point in deep space. It was problematical if he or his crew would ever return.

PLANET OF GHOSTS

By
DAVID V. REED

ARMCHAIR FICTION
PO Box 4369, Medford, Oregon   97501-0168

*For more information about Armchair Books and products, visit our
website at…*

www.armchairfiction.com

Or email us at…

armchairfiction@yahoo.com

CHAPTER ONE
The Call From Space

THE *Flambeau* had stopped. An infinitesimal speck in the measureless void that lies between the worlds that make a universe, it moved like driftwood on a placid sea—a man-made hulk of pale carmine metal hanging in space. Somewhere in the midst of a million miles of darkness it had stopped. The *Flambeau*, pride of the Luxury Fleet of Spaceways, Inc., *was beyond human control.*

In the pitch black of the ether, warm amber light streamed from its thousand portholes like lingering iridescence from the belly of a dying deep-sea fish. Motionless in the sub-frigidity of space, it was a brilliant, beautiful, lifeless thing, its flashing motion halted—a coffin caught between worlds.

Around the navigation desks, the officers of the watch still sat, staring ahead. The Captain lay slumped over his dull metal desk as if he had fallen asleep. In the corridors men and women lay sprawled; the cabins of three decks were filled with humans.

Some of them still sat easily as if they were reading; only the books had in some instances fallen to the floor. There were others half-dressed, lying as if some horrible fatigue had come over them while they were dressing for evening—the arbitrary evening of the eternal night of space, dictated by a clock. The lounge was an immense chamber of silence, its numerous occupants stiff and grotesque, and the third deck, where a late tea had been in progress, as was the custom of Britons, was still spread for tea. People sat around the little tables as if they were waiting...waiting perpetually...

The quiet layover, everything as in a sepulchre, the simultaneous tomb of hundreds, where the lifeless silence lay like a tangible thing. And yet there came a sound, a faint sound!

Dr. Kimball Crane could hear his breath rasping. Air was moving from his lungs, and the sound was raw and uneven. He lay for a time with his head cradled in his arms, slumped against the white surgical table in the *Flambeau's* hospital, remembering. His dark eyes moved slowly over the littered room, seeing the bandages, the overturned bottles, the clean, glistening instruments. Wearily his hand brushed back a dark lock of hair, and the surgeon's cap fell from his head.

He rose weakly to his feet, a tall, slender man, and moved toward the door. Methodically, from the habits of years, he paused to pick up a scalpel—and remembering how he had last used it, he threw it from him in sudden fury.

The clatter followed him through the door. He walked through the corridors trying not to look at the horrible sight that met his eyes, up through the lounge while his steps rang loud and hollow, past the Captain's quarters, up again to the first deck. His step had slowed when he slid open the door to the Communications Cabin.

As he looked about the wrecked interior he fought against despair. He poked his feet about in the mass of torn and broken machinery, and then he was on hands and knees, finding bits of several instruments—etherphones, visiscopes. He was the only man left alive on the *Flambeau*.

Through the long hours that followed as he worked, oblivious to hunger or fatigue, one thought obsessed him. He had no way of knowing where the ship was, and no goal to try to reach with his messages if he ever got them out, but he knew he had to warn others—warn them of what he had seen.

Once or twice he clicked out a trial short-range call, waiting for an answer that might come before he undertook to waste all of the little power he had in one long call.

It was hopeless; he knew that. The automaton sender, the tiny mechanism sealed by the Interplanetary Military Commission, which gave out the secret registry number of the *Flambeau*, had been destroyed. The registry call could not be duplicated by hand. Too well had they provided against counterfeiting registry. Without the identifying call number, anything he sent after that would be disregarded. There were too many ruses current in these troubled days...

But he clung to his hope. He was lost without it. Perhaps with it. He worked over the bits of machines, piecing them together, nursing them, determined to gather enough power for his one effort.

Then, smashing in every crude switch, throwing every last atom of power into his crippled apparatus, he called toward home, calling a number that blazed in his mind. In the deathly stillness the machine whirred and groaned, and the clicks of the sender were sharp little taps of a hammer.

Kimball Crane calling.

He had worked it out so many times in his mind. The machine might go dead at any instant. Whatever got through had to tell the story.

Flambeau lost. Attacked by—

The hand that slid over Crane's was strong. It gripped his fingers and tore them away from the machine.

AROUND the great spaceports of Earth, where the immense charred pits and fields ended, far from the resplendent halls of the terminals, stood the little neat houses run by the Planeteer's Foundation. They were like a tiny fringe clinging to the edge of the only world that meant anything to them—the world of other worlds. There the remnants of man's conquest of space lingered.

Day after day, sitting in the sun, were the men who had once roamed the spaceways. Many of them were old, others were scarred and maimed, but in all of them, even in the most bent and broken of these sailors of the sky, there were evidences of a dignity and belief in themselves and in what had been their calling.

In clear weather they sat and talked, pausing to identify a faint glimmer in the heavens that was a spaceship returning home. Or on foggy days they listened for the burning song of a vessel as it came swinging in through the atmosphere, its hull glowing with heat, a vague luminescence through the mist. It gave them the only peace they knew to sit there and remember.

But sometimes the talk would turn to other things. Sometimes they spoke of the things that only Planeteers knew, odd sights they had seen of the distant wilds to which they had been. And of the legends. For in their time, in the year 2770, when man had been traveling through space for more than four centuries, there were these legends and stories and tales stranger than the imagination. A thousand years before them, earthbound men who sailed the earthbound seas had had their sagas and their legends. Planeteers had theirs.

And what were these legends but nonsense? Any scholarly lad fresh from his extra-territorial geography class could testify to that, or any intelligent layman. There were many people who had sailed millions of miles through the void. As veterans (they always assured one they were veterans) they would hardly pause before they laughed and embarked on a short, pithy discourse on superstition. Nonsense!

And for years the Planeteers had said nothing. To them, jealous as they were of their domain, tired from years of fighting the treacherous, savage void, perhaps they preferred to keep it to themselves.

Then startling things had begun to happen. People didn't like to think about them. But you just couldn't dismiss the vanishing of two space liners on a single day; you had to think about them, because maybe a man you knew had had his family on one of the missing vessels, and it might as easily have been your family.

At first they had blamed these mishaps—totally inexplicable—on the law of averages, on confused theories about cosmic storms, on the usual culprit, the law of probabilities. You could look through the pages of history and find plenty of parallels. Ships had always been lost, and probably always would be, humans being fallible creatures. They were tragedies, doubtless, but what could one do? Not what the alarmists said.

You couldn't cut down on the number of ships; the average lost would be the same. And a highly developed interplanetary commerce had made the Earth as dependent on its colonies as the colonies were on Earth. And one had to remember that scattered throughout the universe were millions of beings that one could call Earthmen only by courtesy. They had been born for generations away from Earth, had lived and died there. They were dependent on Earth for steady supplies, almost all of them even for oxygen to release in their thin atmospheres. Man was the only intelligent life in the universe. Give up his domain?

Hell, no. That was just silly. Who thought of it first, anyhow?

BUT time had passed, and a decade had rolled on since that day when two ships had disappeared on the same day. There had been a brief flurry when some scientist, a Sir Basil Something, had said he discovered both ships had passed a given point and then had been heard from no more. After the flurry, Sir Basil was heard from no more.

Then, in January, 2770, a freighter had come into port towering behind it the scarred and battered hull of the

Sybarite. The *Sybarite* had disappeared three years before. That wasn't what had caused the sensation. It was just that this was the first anyone heard of the *Sybarite* having disappeared in the first place!

Who had hushed it up? How in the world could you hush up a thing like that in this day and age? They had a series of investigations; there were a series of resignations, and somebody laid the blame on inefficiency.

But who was to blame for a certain ship that was even then plowing the ether on its regular run, and named, by happy coincidence, *Sybarite*? Quite a coincidence, too. The ship on the run was an exact duplicate of the missing ship that had turned up! A duplicate! What were they hiding, this nebulous "they" with which the ordinary man referred to those who ran his government?

Scandal somewhere. Illegitimate dealings in contraband, in forbidden drugs. Somebody owned up to it, paid a heavy fine and ended the matter.

A week later there was a fresh sensation. The *City of York* came in to dock with only two fuelers aboard. The rest of the crew and the passengers were gone! And the fuelers were stark, staring mad. They had brought the ship in somehow, by instinct, by some remarkable stroke of luck. But where were the others?

That brought up the *Sybarite* again. There hadn't been anyone aboard her either. Where were they?

The net effect of all this was to bring up the story of Peter Haymes again. He had written about things like this in a book, and the book had sold less than a hundred copies. Of those hundred copies, you couldn't get a single book dealer to own up possessing even one. Laughed right off the market.

The story wasn't funny, however. Peter Haymes had been a big man, the kind they called a captain of industry, wealthy as only a merchant prince of space could be. And what had happened to him? Suicide, or so they said. No one really knew. He had been a man steeped in the cold facts of commerce, an unusual man who poured all his energy and intellect into building an empire. And for relaxation, he had endowed research laboratories, and financed explorations.

And then his young wife and two sons had vanished on the *Flutterby*, his private yacht, a dream of a spaceship. They said it had driven him mad. Sometime after that—it had been in 2765—he had come out with his book, called *Inquiry*.

HAYMES had said all kinds of things in that book. He had gone into exhaustive researches, combed histories. More than that, he had gone among the men who had manned his ships and listened to their talk. He wrote a book that was filled with tales of harpies and fiends and sirens. The sheerest nonsense. Audipress, the universal newscasting agency, used sections of it as humorous news filler. What else could one do with a man who claimed that ten times the number of ships people knew as lost had actually been lost? He told some totally new stories, the one about the *Wanderer*, for instance, a ship that had vanished and returned some twenty years before.

Haymes said that the true story had been hushed up by Military Intelligence. It had returned with all its passengers, three days late, but with some curious quirks among those passengers. They didn't know who they were, they thought they were each other. And it didn't end there. This kind of thing had been going on for a long time, for decades, he said. There were forces at work keeping people in ignorance.

The ridicule had been magnificent. It poured in on him. When he finally disappeared, his empire had tottered from neglect. The creditors and holding companies swarmed over what was left like so many maggots.

The Planeteers had said a few things, referred people to certain pages of *Inquiry*, vouched for their truth, and been laughed at. But that had been five years before, and in the five years other ships had disappeared.

If you spoke to people about it, they assumed the attitude of pioneers. Space was not yet fully conquered and accidents were bound to occur. History showed as much, even Haymes' history. But all through the spring of 2770 the losses were appalling. Traffic fell off. The list of missing ships, never a public document, became a state secret of the first magnitude. Audipress let out some hints about the revival of piracy and the new automatic registry sender was introduced. The restlessness was increasing, but it was kept undercover.

Here and there a person confessed curiosity about Haymes' book. There were open speculations about what was really going on, because by then it was generally assumed that *something* was going on. You couldn't explain so many disappearances—and deaths, constantly increasing, even with the suspected censorship, on history, or any law…

IT WAS the fourth of June that Judd Rafferty got his first clue and lost it. The day was so important to him that it was understandable. On that day he had finished four years as an apprentice in cadet space patrol; he had been given his commission.

He was lieutenant Judd Rafferty of the Interplanetary Military that day, a strong, broad young man with an open, beaming face, very eager, very brave, and a trifle new around the seams. When he looked at people and smiled, with the short-cropped hair rising like a thick brush from his scalp, his uniform uncreased, his boots still creaking, everyone smiled back. June fourth was his day.

But there had been other days. He was scarcely six when he had been put in a state orphanage, with a tiny bank balance marked beside his name. He was eleven when a distant relative came to sign him away to the people who wanted to bring him up as a son. That relative had told him all he knew about his parents. His father had traded in alien plants on distant worlds. When he resolved to give it up and return to his family, his wife had gone to Orion to accompany him home. They were never heard from again. Spaceways, Inc. denied they had booked passage.

From eleven he lived with Captain Schrader and his wife. Both were elderly people and they showered him with affection. Captain Schrader, retired, had spent his life on slow rocket-barges, on tiny freighters, and in his youth, in the monetary exchange vessels that traveled in obsolete armor from colony to colony. Judd Rafferty for ten years lived with a man whose whole life had been his work, and it seemed ordained from all time that when he was old enough, he too would be a planeteer—a real planeteer, not a barge captain. At twenty-one he had entered the cadet space patrols and undertaken the four difficult years. He finished with honors.

The world had begun to smile on Judd Rafferty. He had his commission and his home, and he had his life ahead of him.

The clue came through the first day he was at his desk.

Kmbllcrncllng—dash—*Flmblst*—dash—*ttckb*. It ended there. When it first spluttered weakly through his etherphone, giving no registry number, young Lieutenant Rafferty was very much excited. And then he remembered *Rules and Regulations, Section 12, Paragraph I: Every transmission that is not preceded by a registry number is to be disregarded.* That made sense. The automaton sender never failed. Unregistered calls were for the patrol ships in the vicinity; they would track it down. The young Lieutenant had been taught that people must not be disturbed by meaningless or unauthorized calls. They spread unfounded alarm.

UNDOUBTEDLY, Lieutenant Rafferty would have obeyed regulations if the message had been less obviously cryptic. But there he was at a desk where he would spend a preliminary year. It seemed so prosaic beside the patrol work. The yearning for adventure and romance burned brightly within him. And the message seemed so simple to decode, if indeed code was what it was. He scanned it and saw there were no vowels. Easy enough. *Kmbllcrn*—that was meaningless. But *cllng*, cut off from the rest…could mean *calling*. What had gone before must have been a name.

It hit Rafferty that he wasn't reading a code at all. It was too easy, more like a vowel-sounder on the blink. Could it possibly have been…*Flmlst*… Suddenly he jumped to his feet and dialed in his superior on the office system.

"Lieutenant Rafferty reporting. I have received a somewhat garbled message which seems to say '*Flambeau* lost—attacked by' and then it ends."

The mustache on the superior officer twitched on the screen.

"Have you checked the registry number, Lieutenant?"

"No registry call preceded it, sir."

The mustache stopped twitching.

"Lieutenant, do you remember Section 12, Paragraph 2 of the I. M. bible?"

"Paragraph 2, sir. Yes sir."

There was a black scowl on the screen. He turned and mumbled a few words to someone out of view. The answer came back inaudibly.

"Lieutenant," the officer turned back. "Please tune your visiscope on Double L-3, 900. If that satisfies you, be so good as to report to the discipline committee. I think you ought to find out what Paragraph 2 of the Manual is all about."

"Paragraph 2, sir. Yes sir."

Rafferty had barely time to see the mustache in one final twitch when he dialed. Double L-3, 900. That was the spaceport of Great Chicago. The screen flooded with a view of scarred fields bathed in brutally clear afternoon sun. The sirens were going. Moving the scope about, Rafferty brought a huge, pale rose ship into view. He moved in closer and saw the words *Flambeau*-Luxury Liner, etched in its hull. The under jets were counting off. The roar grew louder.

Lieutenant Rafferty softened the sound until he could hear himself swearing. He knew some picturesque oaths and he combined them all in a long and passionate string. When the afterjets began to count off, he turned off the switch.

So the clue was lost. The day remained important to the young man notwithstanding. It was a major calamity to Lieutenant Rafferty.

Yet Lieutenant Rafferty had had reason to suspect he had lost both his parents in a spaceship. He had been brought up by a man who had often told him strange tales, and he had spent many an afternoon among the Planeteers. In his mind and heart he was already a Planeteer.

The clue, nevertheless, slipped through his fingers. And that was understandable.

CHAPTER TWO
Death Ship

"SO YOU'VE come back!" Dr. Kimball Crane had cried out in astonishment, but he might have cried in pain. The pressure on his own strong hands was unrelenting, crushing his fingers. The fatigue of hours was sucking insistently at his strength, and the room was moving in a slight, uneven arc;

the three men before him, dim, bulky figures in heavy ether-tunics were moving with it, and the effort of thought had become too much...

Someone was slapping his face, and Crane knew he had fainted. An empty, folded ether-tunic was lying near him and he heard the mumbled instructions to get into it. He struggled with the heavy fibre-cloth.

When he rose, from a porthole he could see the dark, slender form of the ship that had hailed the *Flambeau* hours before. He followed the men heavily, every step difficult. There was a merciful mist before his eyes that blotted out the horror that lay on all sides.

Outside the final lock, one of the men pushed off and seemed to float down to a waiting tender. Crane followed, but there was so little strength left in him that his push didn't quite make it. He hung for a moment in free space. Will the astronomers find me, he was thinking incoherently. Maybe a liner would smash into him and spread him like a thin film over its hull. An odd death, he was thinking. Where were they taking him?

The next moment the two following men had leaped and pulled his inert form with them into the tender. It moved away slowly, propelled by short bursts of compressed air.

They were edging down the gangway when Crane realized he was on a fighting ship. Silver-duct lines to supply heat rays hung so low he had to stoop, and firing coils, and sliding metal shields. But this was no regular Military ship, and pirates—pirates didn't do what Crane had seen.

Then he heard it again—and he had wished never to live to hear it ever again. A low, sibilant cry that was half moan and half sigh, as if all the world had joined their voices in a great dirge and the sound had carried through all of space to penetrate to him.

There was something in the sound that was wild and yet subdued, like a wail of protest, when the protest was useless. There was grief in it, a vast insane sadness. Its note vibrated in a human ear and ran through the body until the bones returned the vibration in sympathy. There was something complete and universal in the sound, and it brought a flood of memories, unknown and unrecognizable, whirling through the brain.

Crane shook as if he had been in the throes of a violent, alien fever, and he saw the bodies of the men with him trembling. Then it was gone and they went forward again.

When they stopped again, Crane knew he was in the commanding officer's quarters. This was the chartroom, sparsely furnished, the walls covered with calculation tables, travel arcs, astronomical configuration maps. A massive burnished copper desk stood in a corner, a deep tan rug covered the floor, and there were several chairs. Crane sat in silence while the men stood quietly, emerging from their helmets, paying him no attention. Crane was grateful for the respite. He closed his eyes, trying to relax.

AFTER a time he sensed a movement in the room. He opened his eyes to see a man walk into the room. He was dressed in ordinary blue coveralls, somewhat stained by grease and open at the neck. Beyond a little red skullcap that he wore, there was no mark of authority on him, no symbol to convey rank. That stood out sharply from his manner, from his lithe step, from his deliberate wave of an arm to the men in the room. He was tall and angular, and his features were not immediately discernible because of a short, thick beard he wore, as dark as the mat of hair over his great forehead, and his eyes shone with a hard, brilliant blueness.

"Thank you," he said. The men left the room.

The bearded man sat down on one end of the desk, much as a schoolboy might, and regarded Crane.

"I hadn't thought we'd meet again, Doctor." His voice was deep, his manner informal but polite. He added, "You've put me to a great deal of trouble."

"No more than the trouble to which you put me."

"Does the knowledge that you saved my life distress you so much? It shouldn't. But for that, you might now be among the dead on the *Flambeau*."

"You might have given me my choice."

"Unfortunately, that choice also affected my life." The bearded man smiled a bit. "Venusian swamp fever is easy to fight with the proper medicines. I am already recovered as you see. But believe me, Dr. Crane, what happened to the *Flambeau* was not in my plans when I hailed it."

"The wanton killing of hundreds by your men—"

"Please," the man interrupted. "My men did nothing. You came to the scene a bit late to discover what actually happened, but as a doctor you must have noticed—surely you noticed—something odd, shall we say, about the manner in which death came to those people. No heat incisions, no blueness of electric bolts. I am as anxious to escape notoriety at this moment as the authorities on Earth seem to be anxious to help that desire. Their adherence to an age-old policy pleases me. I would not have done anything like mass murder at this time. For many reasons."

Crane said suddenly, "I know you. I've known you somewhere...I can't remember. But somewhere...if I could think."

"You see," said the other, after a momentary pause, "what a risk I run by sparing your life out of a gallant gratitude? I left you once with only a fractional chance of returning to life, and I had hardly left when my ship picked up the experimental calls you sent. You pressed the best speed from my ship, but I believe we returned in time. What went through will undoubtedly be discarded." He paused a moment. "You hardly know, Dr. Crane, the condition of Earth's interplanetary traffic, nor of the fantastic measures they have had to take in the past few years. Few men know. I find it a welcome condition."

Crane was looking at the man. There was a prominent blue vein that ran the length of his forehead. His nose was well shaped, his chin was firm. Without the beard he would have been a handsome man of some fifty years, although there was scarcely a gray hair on him. But Crane couldn't remember. Fatigue was drinking his strength. The sound of his own voice, like the other's, seemed to come from far off.

"Unrest poisons your mind, Doctor," said the man. "I will put you at ease. We of this ship are pirates—yes. But we are not the anachronistic freebooters of another age. Our prize is an exceptional one, and our equipment for the task finds no equal in man's most haunted dreams. You have fallen into the orbit of a plan, like the brief comet wasting itself, and soon you will be gone." He softened his tone, seeing the luster in Crane's eyes, knowing how tired the other was. "'If you are unfortunate, and live, you may come to see things beyond your understanding. You may come to wish that I had never spared your life."

Crane's voice was a sigh, weak and distant. "I know who...you are...Peter Haymes..."

WHEN Crane rose from the bed on which he had been lying, he saw by the interstellar clock that he had slept for more than twelve hours. He sat by the large amberglass porthole and looked out into the dark splendor of the universe. In outer space the starry worlds took on a new character, without the miles of dust-laden atmosphere to dim their glory, they emerged anew, often with faint colors to stud the black heavens like a handful of scattered gems.

So three days passed…

Sometimes Crane read from a small stack of books in his room. Sometimes he played with the music recorder. But most of the time he lay quietly in the darkness and thought. Peter Haymes…

He had never met him, but he had seen and heard him countless times on the visiscope—at the commencement of a college; laying the foundation for a structure; making speeches; being interviewed. He had been missing for almost five years. Where had he been all that time? What had he been doing?

Perhaps people should have guessed that he was alive, somewhere. He wasn't the kind to have bowed before adversity. Not he. All his life he had fought, within the rules and without, but savagely and well. His memory was a monument to that, in spite of the sorry ending. But it hadn't ended. Haymes had come through that horrible chapter—for it was evident now that it had been but a chapter. What would this brilliant man write into the story of his life before he was through? What next?

On the third day, Haymes came to Crane. He waved his hand in half familiarity and sat down across the room from Crane. His expression was calm and thoughtful as he lit a Mercurian cigarette and offered the luxury to his guest. Then, not until both men had exhaled the last of it did Haymes break the silence.

"You shouldn't have told me you knew who I was," he said. "It…uh…complicates matters. Even mercy can be misguided."

"Mercy seems to play a small part in your life."

"For an excellent reason, Doctor," Haymes agreed, passively. "If you know me, you must know what I have suffered. But I can hardly expect you to understand. The men who are tied to me by the greatest of all bonds—blind loyalty—they will be repaid. The others…" he lit another cigarette before he completed the sentence, "…likewise repaid."

"What can you hope to accomplish alone, no matter how well armed?"

"Alone?" Haymes smiled. "Hardly. This ship is but part of my organization. There are men in my employ on Earth and on many of its colonies, some in positions that put them beyond suspicion—if, indeed, there is any suspicion."

"If your intention is to taunt me with subtleties and hints," said Crane, "consider yourself a success. I haven't the vaguest idea of what you mean. But it seems to me that you are suffering from certain delusions of grandeur. As a doctor to a patient, I might say to you that these dreams of yours, obviously of revenge, can bring you nothing but further sorrow.

"You interest me, Doctor. Go on." Haymes face had grown dark. The muscles of his jaw flicked as he controlled his anger.

"I should charge you a handsome fee for this," said Crane, indulging in a smile that he knew must prove intensely irritating. "I was previously an army surgeon and had little occasion for psychiatric work. Your case history, if I may call it such, began when you lost those dearest to you. Tragic as it was, what happened to you was worse. For you lost your most prized possession—your mind. And you wandered to strange activity which could only result in merited ridicule—"

"Merited?" Haymes had jumped to his feet. He spat the word out. "I'll show you how merited it was! There—"

A soft knock on the door interrupted him. It opened and one of Haymes' men stood there. "We've entered the white area," he said.

HAYMES nodded and dismissed him. But when he turned again to Crane, he had regained his composure. The interruption had quieted him.

"You're playing a rather obvious game, Doctor," he said.

"What do you expect to gain by angering me?"

"I don't know yet," Crane replied easily. "Maybe I want a look at something I missed on the *Flambeau*. I am very much interested in that new weapon of yours."

"You almost got me to show it to you. Sorry."

Crane returned the other's pleasantry.

"There will be another time," Crane observed. "The best thing about your kind of madness is that the ego demonstrates itself even when it knows better. You'll slip again."

Haymes was forcing himself to remain calm again.

"I'm afraid there won't be time enough to disprove you," he said. "We are nearing your last destination. Look out of the porthole."

Crane turned and stared out. He could see nothing but a blank whiteness. It had no dimensions, no depth, no form. It was as if the ship had been immersed in a sea of milk except for the fact that there was not even a suggestion of liquidity about the whiteness. A dead white—nothing more.

"Your headquarters?" said Crane.

"You might say so. Temporarily, at any rate. I expect to shift to more commodious and familiar headquarters very soon. The Earth, say."

"You sound like some sinister, if outmoded, dictator," Crane laughed. "We outgrew dictators centuries ago. You sound slightly ridiculous."

"All right, Dr. Crane." Haymes' fists were tightly clenched. "I don't know what stops me from killing you here and now—"

"Your ego," Crane smiled. "It won't let you because I'm the first fresh audience you've had in a long time. You've got to prove something to me, to show me how right you are and what a fool I am."

"Right again! Interpret this as a victory if you like. I am going to show you what a fool you are. Please follow me."

Making no attempt to hide his amusement, Crane followed Haymes out of the room and down a narrow corridor to Haymes' quarters. Playing this game of intellectual teasing was working. Where it would end was a matter of conjecture. Crane would find out what he could before he thought of any way out, if there was any way. Remembering what had happened to the *Flambeau* made his own salvation unimportant somehow. He had to get out word of Haymes, to send a warning. He was playing for that.

As if the past few moments had resulted in an inbreeding of his anger, Haymes turned to Crane with his face a dull red.

"Stand beside me, Doctor, and don't move if you value your life." He opened a drawer of his desk and took from it a small tubular object a foot in length. Then he slid out a panel board from the desk on which were rows of buttons, each marked with some section of the ship. He held his finger over one marked *C. Q.*, probably to correspond with *Captain's Quarters*, and flashed a savage grin at Crane.

"The answer to a thousand questions," he said quietly, and pressed his finger down.

THE only noticeable change was very slight, Crane thought. It had completely escaped his attention until then. The room, as the whole ship had been, was bathed in some vaguely greenish light, so slight as to be imperceptible. Crane had been too tired to notice it when he had come aboard, and probably he had grown so accustomed to the slight change that it had never occurred to him. But now, as Haymes' finger pressed down the *C. Q.* button, the green light in the room faded away and was made noticeable by its sudden absence. Immediately afterward the room was plunged into complete darkness.

Then Crane heard the moaning, heard it grow louder. In spite of his courage, his body was racked by great shudders of uncontrollable fear. It was the sound he had heard twice before, the same completely terrifying and inhuman cry that had driven him almost insane.

Through the walls there slowly coalesced the first of three figures—moving through solid substance and coming toward them. They were perhaps three feet high—but they were transparent, ghostlike, fragile as the figures in a dream, with half their outlines obliterated and the rest like grayish, gold-flecked smoke against the black of darkness.

Crane knew then the utter agony of pure fear, felt it bursting his heart, in the hammers that were pounding in his temples, in the hot bath of his sweat. Some power that was not his own kept his consciousness when he pleaded for oblivion, some strength held him on his feet when he knew he could no longer endure.

Closer and closer the figures came, wheeling about in a circular motion, and Crane imagined he saw traceries of features on them. Closer and closer still. And then something beside Crane lit up in the darkness, a thin beam of light, pale green, like a bright knife cutting its way through the dark. It stabbed each of the three figures quickly.

The next moment the wailing reached a crescendo—and the figures suddenly fled!

The cylinder in Haymes' hand, its light faintly illumining his tightly clenched fingers, went dark. A switch clicked into position and the room lit up. The figures were gone; the sounds had ended.

Crane stumbled to a chair and flung himself into it. Haymes stood near him.

"Have I satisfied you?" he asked, softly. "Do my words still sound empty to you? That was what you missed on the *Flambeau*—the death of your fellow passengers at the hands of...my weapon. And the answer, the only defense? Locked in here." He returned the cylinder to his desk. "And in here." He pointed to his temples. "A pirate with imagination and ambition enough could take the world with it."

"What was it?" Crane found it difficult to speak.

Haymes shrugged.

"Diagnose that answer, if you can."

"What do you intend to do with it...with them?"

"Them is correct, Doctor. There were several hundred clustered about my ship when I hailed the *Flambeau* for your serum. I intended using them on worthy game, say, military ships. Unfortunately they got out of hand and you saw the result. They were all—how shall I put it—used up? That's as good an answer as any. So I had to return here for more. You might call this their home. Shall we...ah...call them ghosts?"

Kimball Crane sat quietly. In his experience he had heard other men speak as Haymes was speaking. Perhaps it was the suffering that had taken its toll. He had heard the evidence once in a stifled sob when Haymes had mentioned his bitterness. But this was no mere madman. There was a deadly undercurrent in him. Peter Haymes was a hideously warped man inside; there were scars deep inside him that had never healed, etched in an acid that had tortured him and eaten into his being. Now, bemused, he looked at Crane and spoke again.

"You may be interested, Dr. Crane, to know the fate I have stored for you. The destination I spoke of, meaning yours, and the home of these...uh...ghosts, are really the same place. They come from a planet above which we happen now to be. You, Doctor, are going to live on that planet…"

IF Haymes had expected any overt reaction from Crane, he was disappointed. Crane didn't move a muscle. The reaction was all inside him. He knew now that his own life was ended. There was something he had to do before he was through. He was even then scanning the wall charts, and his eyes were fixed on one of them that had a trail of pins marked on it, pins that started with the location, the last location, of the *Flambeau*, and continuing in a bright line toward nowhere. The last pin marked a spot in space.

If, as in all interplanetary ships, the charts were marked from hour to hour, then they were now nowhere at all. Yet Haymes was saying something quite different. Crane looked down along the sides of the chart, to the guidelines, memorizing their tale. To what end, he told himself, looking at the silent Haymes again.

"Thank you for the entertainment," Crane said presently. "And now, if you don't mind, shall we be going?"

"Afraid you'll be late?" said Haymes, leading the way out. "I didn't make any appointment for you."

"My only regret," said Crane, following Haymes down the corridor, wondering at the prodigious strength of the ship as its armaments revealed, "is at having to call on these strangers without a shave."

The light pat of their footsteps on the metal floor punctuated the conversation as they moved to the aft of the ship. At the end of the corridor, at their approach a large circular door slid open to admit them. Two of the crew were inside, and Crane saw that they had come to a combination storeroom and shell chamber. There were half a dozen of the collapsible, one-man shells in which gunners could go out alone to circle their prey like deadly gnats, and Haymes pointed to one of these.

"Guns out, sir," said one of the men. "Two cartridges of compressed air loaded. Ready to go this minute."

Haymes turned to Crane.

"That's for you, you know. I'm sorry we won't be able to escort you all the way."

Crane nodded absently. Two cartridges of compressed air would give the tiny shell about two hours of motive power, and for two hours he could wander about in space, in that strange whiteness outside. But he was more concerned with other things he saw. There were fully twenty 12-inch heat-bore guns, many others of smaller bore, insulated battle armor, electric bolt rifles, hand weapons. Overhead were fixed lifeboats, cables for towing back spent shells. And there were two etherphones...

"Any last request?" said Haymes. "I like formalities."

"Got any cigarettes?"

"Certainly." From his tunic, Haymes withdrew his box of cigarettes and handed them over. "Anything else?"

Crane had dropped the box. In stooping to retrieve it he accidentally kicked it away, and he went after it. When he rose again, his hand had reached out and seized one of the hand weapons. He wheeled and faced the men with the heat pistol in his hand.

"Just thought of it," he said, quietly. "There's someone I'd like to ask to take care of my canaries. Pick up one of those etherphones!"

"WHERE do you think this is going to get you?" Haymes countered. "The only men aboard who didn't carry sidearms are in this room, because we didn't like the idea of you snatching one of them. But there are guns enough outside to fry you to a turn."

"You aren't outside. You're here with me, and I'm quite willing to fry you before the chef reaches me."

Haymes lowered one of his raised hands to stifle a yawn.

"An interesting notion," he said. "Call me in the morning."

"Pick up that etherphone!" said Crane. "You've got half a minute."

Fifteen seconds went by before Haymes spoke.

"Crane, you can't operate that phone and keep us covered at the same time. You can't shoot us because you don't know where the outlet for the phone is. And none of us are going to send out your damned message and be shot down a minute later. You can kill me, all right, but what of my organization? There are men who know almost as much as I know. They'll take over."

Part of that, at least, was true. The worst that could happen to Haymes was his own death; it would be the end of the universe for him. But that would scarcely be any comfort to Crane, if it was true that he had an organization. If the thought of death terrified Haymes still he would not send out a message knowing that the same death awaited him. There was no time; someone might come up at any moment. And there was a warning that had to be sent...

"You know I'm right," said Haymes. "I'll make a bargain with you. I want your word that if we send your message, you'll not harm us."

"You have my word. Get the etherphone."

Crane kept his eyes fixed on the man who lifted the heavy instrument, watching him set it on the floor. He moved aside two crates and lifted a ring. Underneath lay the glistening red glass of the outlet. The man plugged in the etherphone and he sat down beside it.

"Rattle it," said Crane.

The hammer tripped off *tic-tic-tic*. It was in order.

"Adjust it to 2,000 revs. Right. Signal the number I. M. 50. Right. Now take this. 'Dr. Kimball Crane calling. I am the only survivor of the *Flambeau*, which was attacked in space by the pirate craft of Peter Haymes. He is alive and has new and dangerous weapons at his disposal. I am calling from his craft, position approximately J-J 54, point 55.03, point 7. I am about to be marooned here. Warn all Military ships. That is all.' "

CRANE watched the corners of Haymes mouth curl up.

"What about registry?" said Haymes. "What do you think they'll do about a call without a registry number?"

"Send it again," said Crane to the crewman. "I'm listening and I know the code. Send it again."

But the repeat was barely started when a voice piped through the intership communications horn.

"Shell room. Observation calling. Engine room reports ship idling. Have you fired the shell?"

Crane moved his gun.

"Tell him it's going off in a minute." Haymes moved to the mouthpiece of the horn, switched it in.

"Any minute now." He paused for an instant, then added, "Order all hands to guns. Get ready for a coverall broadside." He switched off and turned back to Crane. "We're going to make it interesting for you to get away," he smiled. "That heat gun makes you a dangerous man."

Crane hardly heard him, intent as he was on listening to the ether-phone ticking off the message…

Presently Crane looked up.

"All right, now. Stand back against the wall." The three men retreated to the door. With one hand Crane pushed back the catches on the shell. A swift glance through a porthole disclosed nothing but the whiteness, that queer, uncanny white. Silently he donned the head mask that lay nearby, tested the oxygen discharge. The controls were set, the shell was on its stays, the fuse was a long, ugly black string. He kneeled beside it and bit it in half with his teeth.

A risky business, that short fuse, but no more risky than waiting for it to go off while Haymes and his two crewmen were there to stop it. As if there was any difference in dying aboard the ship or outside.

He slid into the seat of the shell backward. With a sudden motion he flipped on a torch against the fuse and whipped the cover down on the shell.

Almost instantaneously there was a crashing in his ears, a lurch that tore at his viscera. He was free of the ship!

Swiftly he slid back the amberglass visor in the cover of the shell and looked out. The white had become grayish, undulating shapes, like masses of huge clouds, or like steam that had been made into a more stable almost viscous, form.

Waiting for the first crackling, hissing sound of the plates when the black ship would fire, Crane sat tense at the controls, keeping a perfectly straight course.

A straight course where?

His journey to nowhere had begun.

CHAPTER THREE
Disclosure

LIEUTENANT Rafferty had been disciplined. He had sat quietly before the military commission and listened to Captain Andrews, he of the twitching mustache.

"I find, Lieutenant," the Captain had said, "that you have a penchant for melodrama and adventure, and that you are determined to hunt it right at your own desk. You can't sit still, Lieutenant. Ants in your pants, or too many vitamins in your breakfast. So we're going to cure you. Military Intelligence has been short handed all year, and has requested us to transfer suitable officers. We consider you a first class rocket bomb, and accordingly find you suitable for service with the M. I. staff. Effective immediately."

New as he was in the service, Judd Rafferty hardly appreciated the sarcasm in Captain Andrew's words. Interplanetary Military Intelligence, the I. M. I., or M. I., was a burial ground no matter how it was abbreviated; the final resting place of officers who played the wrong politics. One could easily understand this. The function of M. I. was to listen, sort and record grievances of passengers in interplanetary traffic, adjust the petty quarrels of shippers, arrange schedules, and carry on the office routine incident to police work on mandated planets and colonies. The M. I. was nursemaid to the problems of commerce.

But Lieutenant Rafferty reacted strangely. He was certain he would find fascination in the work that left others weary with boredom. Man had found no other intelligent life in the universe, but man had so much variation within himself, that, added to generations of breeding and living on distant worlds, he had peopled the universe with new beings. Rafferty had met many of these people before, when as a boy in his teens, they had come to visit his guardian, Captain Schrader. Then they had captured his heart and mind and imagination. He had spoken to people who had never seen the Earth before, whose forefathers had been born on distant stars, and he had listened to the tales they had poured out.

It was to the unending line of these people that Rafferty now looked forward to meeting again. For some reason, the tales he had heard from them, and the stories of the Planeteers, when of an afternoon he and the Captain had walked among them—all these things were suddenly, constantly on his mind. He wanted to hear how other people spoke again. He remembered that they had seemed to act differently—to think differently; their minds, like the minds of all people reared in semi-civilized habitats, seemed childlike and poetic and free in many ways. They spoke of strange forms of life, of inexplicable happenings...

NOT even the first day at his post discouraged him. A foppish and lackadaisical Major had lectured several new men on their duties. The main thing was discipline. They were to listen to people and have the entire interviews recorded on dictascopes, an apparatus that took down conversations and photographed those concerned in them, all on tiny rolls of film. These film records and accompanying soundtracks were each day to be given to the officers from the files.

That was all. With the recording, duty ended. But the Major took it upon himself to supplement the lecture with a few side remarks. He had spun a little swagger stick in his hands and said.

"You will notice there is no compulsion to take these matters seriously. Quite the other way, in fact. M. I. expects all of you to keep a sense of balance, even a sense of the ridiculous, you might say. It won't do to keep flying off the handle about everything you hear. And you will find that among experienced M. I. men, most of what you will hear are classified as 'screwball sagas.' "

The Major had snickered, and the new men snickered with him. All except Rafferty. Curiously enough, the speech had a chastening effect on him, and it left him rather subdued. Which may have been intended.

But whatever malign and relentless fate was pursuing Lieutenant Rafferty—if indeed it was not merely his childishness dignified with another name—that fate was not to be put off. Having begun by putting Rafferty under disciplinary restraint on his first day of duty in the corps, it marked time briefly and catapulted him into another situation from which there was no retreat.

It was three days after he had taken up his new post that Rafferty listened to a man from New Pleiptes. He was a tanned, weather-beaten planter, and in his direct manner, he told of how he had ordered machines months before, and how they had come late. And again he had ordered several motor plows and received a promise that they would arrive on time.

"Had two hundred men waitin' for the stuff," he complained angrily, "and I find out a couple of days ago that they'll be three weeks late. What the hell is going on around here?"

"This is hardly a matter for the M. I.," said Rafferty. "It seems to me that you have an insurance claim for delay against the liner."

"Damned right I have!" the planter had spluttered. "And they paid off fast. They always pay fast. But I want an explanation. I tried to talk about it to the Spaceways people and they shut me up. All they said was, 'What ship was it, please?' and when I answered, 'The *Flambeau*,' they signed my claim."

"Did you say *Flambeau?*" said Rafferty. "When was this?"

"Last few days. The *Flambeau* was supposed to pick up the plows at Church's planet, where they'd been sent before. Instead I'm goin' to get 'em on a direct shipment from Chicago."

"On what vessel?"

"The *Flambeau*, of course."

"Of course."

THE matter ended there officially. Lieutenant Rafferty called Spaceways and found that the *Flambeau* had reported in early, and as a consequence, its schedule had been altered. Rafferty soothed the planter diplomatically. And when he was through, he sat back and wondered who in hell was going to soothe him. Because he needed soothing, because he was powerless to check the absolutely insane, weird thoughts he was thinking.

Or perhaps it was that young Rafferty had been caught in a swift, tragic swirl of events that carried him helpless in a raging tide. The events make the man as much as men make events. It took the quick—inordinately quick—juxtaposition of connected events and the peculiar man that Rafferty was, considering his temperament and background, to make him do what he did that day.

It was then the end of a Friday, when things were at odds because of the impending weekend. One of the M. I. officers from the filing vaults had come through, steering the huge, portable wagon-cases in which all new records were taken up before they were finally added to the old batch. When Rafferty first looked up, there was a case standing near his desk. It was unattended.

That was enough to arouse his curiosity, for from what he had seen of the cases, they were never left alone even for an instant. Headquarters seemed to prize those cases. And this particular case had been the subject of several conversations that afternoon—rather excited ones, with men running around and whispering and acting important.

It seemed an odd way to act about records that no one gave a hang about when they were being gathered by junior officers. Especially when one remembered that the same man never took the same case twice in succession, and that inside the vaults there were other switches of men, and the actual filing, they said, was finally done by ranking officers.

But there it was alone, after all that silly confusion. And it did not occur to Rafferty at first that he was interested. He was just standing there, running his hands idly over the containers. There were innumerable small metal boxes in the case, each holding a thousand or so feet of film record. But suddenly, he caught himself.

He had been playing, unconsciously certainly, with the shelf marked "F", and he had seen where his interview with the planter had been placed. But well to the rear of it, deep inside the case, there was a long, flat box marked, "Unregistered Calls." That was what stopped him short...

He had surmised, of course, that some sort of record had to be kept even of those calls, but now as he thought about it, he wondered at the special attention given to messages that M. I. was officially supposed to ignore. Why should they be preserved?

Was there perhaps a record of the call that had come to him four days before—the call that had disciplined him right out of ship-contact calls to Intelligence work? And why keep ship-contact calls with the dictascope records? What connection could there be between them?

Almost inadvertently he had been taking the box from the case—then all at once he knew what he was going to do. He opened the box, took out the film roll and placed it in his own dictascope, then released the switch that allowed the playback to operate.

THERE was a soft *tic-tic-tic* as the machine began, and then came the voice. Etherphones, the only means of communication in space, sent only letters in signal codes, but here they had been transposed and were enunciated either as letters or as whole words. The code letters impinged on the Stewart diaphragm, and it transposed it vocally.

Kmbllcrncllng—dash—*Flmblst*—dash—*ttckb*. That was what Rafferty heard. So they had really preserved the call. It didn't make sense. The voice came on, enunciating the date on which the message had been received. Rafferty leaned over to turn off the switch, when he heard the *tic-tic-tic* again. Was it going to repeat?

But the next moment Rafferty's hair was trying to stand on end as he listened. There was a numbness all through him.

Dr. Kimball Crane calling. I am the only survivor of the Flambeau, which was attacked in space by the pirate craft of Peter Haymes. He is alive and has new and dangerous weapons at his disposal. I am calling from his craft, position approximately J-J 54, point 55.03, point 7. I am about to be marooned here. Warn all Military ships. That is all.

The thin, ticking noise followed briefly, then the voice added: *Unregistered call received at ship-contact post. York Headquarters of Interplanetary Military, June 8, 2770. 4:21 P. M. End.*

How long he sat there, slumped in his seat and unable to move, Judd Rafferty had no way of knowing; all he remembered later was that things had been going on inside him, half-thoughts flashing by, innumerable vague ideas like images from the distant past, and they were tearing him apart. Over and over there was a little crazy refrain in his head. It kept making *Kmbllcrncllng* mean something. *Kimball Crane,* it kept singing...

There was a hand on his shoulder, gripping him fiercely. Behind Rafferty stood a burly Lieutenant—the officer in charge of the violated filing case!

"Get away from that desk," he shouted to Rafferty.

His fist had come up about halfway when Rafferty caught him. There was no rage in Rafferty. There was unfinished business that he had to attend. His actions were almost methodical, in spite of his swiftness. He caught the other's arm and twisted, and there had scarcely been a cry of pain when Rafferty's blow smashed into the other's face. The officer went down in a heap and lay there.

Rafferty's voice was thin as he spoke into the visiscope.

"Central Hospitals? Lieutenant Rafferty. Official business, Military Intelligence. Please check on a Dr. Kimball Crane. His last movements."

An interminable half-minute went by. Then—

"Dr. Crane left Earth on January 12, aboard the *Firefly*. He was due back June sometime—hold on—this week, aboard the *Flambeau*, having reported his intention of returning in an official capacity. There is a blank here to indicate that he has not yet reported. There seems to be... A notation came in some hours ago. Dr. Crane is reported engaged in special fieldwork outside communications range in an infected area. Is there anything else?"

"No," said Rafferty. "Thank you." It added up...it kept adding up.

And then Rafferty saw for the first time that the officer who had been on the floor wasn't there! He had sneaked out silently. It was a matter of minutes now. Less. He could hear the intra-office sirens going on. There was nothing to do but wait...

COMMANDER Scott leaned back in his chair and opened his snuffbox. The little black flakes of dust had left their mark on the white gloves on his hands. Slowly his hand brought the snuff up to his nose. It was a long, slender nose, cruel looking. Everything about the Commander was cruel looking. His face was thin and dark as a hawk's, his short wiry body seemed stooped and crooked, his sparse hair covered a large, irregular skull. And the gloves, unblemished white except for the snuff marks, snapping imperious fingers, concealing the iron hand of Scott that was dreaded throughout the service.

"You've had quite a day, Lieutenant," said Scott. "Why won't you tell me about it?" His milky gray eyes were piercing as his fingers drummed on the table. "What have you found out?" he said. And all at once he smashed a hand down and shouted, "Answer me, Lieutenant!"

"There's nothing to answer." Judd Rafferty sounded weary. He had been waiting for hours for Commander Scott. He had expected court martial and drumming out; instead he had waited until Scott came, and now the two of them sat quite alone in his chambers. Outside the night had fallen, and from nearby the brilliant beacons of the spaceport flashed in the sky like pale, searching fingers. "It isn't that I don't want to tell you," Rafferty added. "It's just that I don't know what I know."

Commander Scott turned away.

"Go on," he said.

"I can't go on. I don't know anything. The service has fixed things so that we can't know anything. All we can do is think—those of us who have things to think about, and there aren't many." He paused, and suddenly the words poured out of him. "When I first got that message from Dr. Crane, I thought it meant something. It looked like a vowel sounder out of commission. The same thing that ruined the vowel sounder could have ruined the automaton registry sender, even though we were told the senders never fail. Then Captain Andrews showed me the *Flambeau* at the spaceport in Chicago. That stopped me...then."

"Indeed?" Quietly. Then Scott said, "Say it, Lieutenant."

It was as if Scott had been waiting for him, knowing what he had to say, and waiting.

"I'll say it." Rafferty's voice was even. "I think the ship I saw in Chicago was a double for the *Flambeau*. I think there have been other ships with doubles..." His voice trailed off.

THE room was a silent island in the midst of an ocean of noise. Rafferty could hear the noise outside, beating like waves on a beach, moving in the streets below, carrying life past him. But here there was nothing. He and Scott alone. And the silence, thin as a thread lost in infinity, stretching away beyond knowledge.

Presently Scott leaned forward in his chair, and held his hands out to Rafferty.

"Look at my hands, Lieutenant!" His voice was soft now, but under it Rafferty could feel the heat of emotion. "I wear gloves to hide the ghastly scars on them. There are scars one can hide more easily, yet wear less comfortably."

He sank back to his seat and breathed slowly. When he spoke again, it was without visible effort, as if he was reminiscing out loud.

"When I was your age, I was mate on a small mail tender. I got the scars on that tender's last voyage, escaping in a lifeboat. I had to get out so fast my hands stuck in one of the locks. But the records say I wasn't aboard on that voyage. The records say I was behind in the hospital because of acid burns on both hands. And the records say the tender continued in service. Or, as you say—*its double*. Because I saw that ship lose every man aboard, and go hurtling down to the surface of some obscure planet. The crew? Supposedly dispersed throughout the merchant marine; a new crew was aboard on the next trip. Check on them if you can get the records. The insurance was paid in time, on those who had people to claim it. That was a long time after it all happened."

"You mean—" Judd Rafferty said, incredulously.

"I mean there are things we don't talk about…"

Scott's face was drained of color as he rose and walked to a window.

"I learned not to talk when I came back. I joined the service, and on the first of these little stars on my uniform— one for each year in the I. M.—there was a little field of red. Have you ever seen those stars, Lieutenant, and wondered why that red field was worn by some men? *It indicates the year in which the man had to be told.* And now you must be told. There are few men with the red field, scarcely any with the field on the first star. Your background, perhaps, or imagination, circumstances…"

The Commander waved an arm as he dismissed the possibilities. He came back to his desk.

"Lieutenant, rumors are seldom dangerous—as long as they stay rumors. If your knowledge was common, our liners would gather dust in the spaceports. Our people scattered throughout the universe might be cut off from each other. Those who live by our supplies would die horrible deaths. Our interplanetary intercourse, on which so much of our own life depends, would be at an end."

Slowly Rafferty asked, "What is it that's doing this to us? What enemy have we, what force?"

Scott laughed shortly and dryly.

"Our secret archives have recorded these things for a century and a half. What is there, Lieutenant? No one knows. So no one must ask. But we've kept forging ahead, because we have to. Because we fear that if we stop going out to meet this unknown danger—it may come down to meet us!"

"But the message," said Rafferty. "It involved Peter Haymes."

"Haymes hasn't been alive for five years," said Scott. "So that even if we are willing to believe that he is alive now, and that he let a prisoner use his etherphone for some reason, how would that explain the things that happened so long ago? No, the answer lies elsewhere. We have drawn charts and diagrams by the thousand. One thing we know. The catastrophes have been occurring closer to Earth, and they have been multiplying so quickly that it is only a matter of time until the general public finds out that thousands are missing—in these past few months alone. The day they find out will be a sad day indeed. And it is against that day that our elaborate secrecy is directed.

"We have been taking our chances, employing doubles, giving them unregistered call phones, listening to their reports. Nothing has come of it. So we keep on. Those we lose are involuntary sacrifices for the safety and security of the rest of the world, and the other worlds. Inhuman? But how else can we find out who our enemy is—or what it is? We must find out, not here but in space, and we must fight it in space, away from our loved ones. Or else we may all perish. But until we know...silence..."

"The Planeteers talk of things..." Rafferty began.

"We know them all. They crowd our records. But we must laugh at those who get too many notions, unless we can give them a red field around their service stars. We must sneer! But the *Flambeau*, like the many who went before it, like my little mail tender, has not been forgotten. And though we make rules to preserve secrecy, we cannot forget. Here..."

THE Commander bent over a visiscope and tuned. The large wall screen behind him lit up, then abruptly blacked out. A military official appeared on the screen; he saluted and faded. In his place rose one of the interiors of Central Hospitals, and the screen took in a sweep of corridors and moved toward a guarded series of doors. Here again the visiscope was challenged and passed, and on the screen appeared the inside of an enormous chamber, which for all its size, was carefully secreted.

There were triplex arrangements of rooms within, and dozens of people moving about, or sitting with doctors speaking to them. The visiscope moved closer, toward a small group.

A short blond man was saying, "I'm James Harmon. This fellow is Harry Parks. Have you got it straight now?"

"But your passports say you are Parks and he is Harmon," said the Doctor, gently. "The photographs bear out this contention."

The man beside the short one spoke up.

"He's crazy, Doc. He must have switched the photographs with somebody. Probably a crook. And I wish you'd stop humoring him by calling me Harmon. Donald Ferris is a good enough name for me. I never saw this guy before."

The doctor shook his head. From a pocket he withdrew a hand mirror and showed it to the man who had spoken last. Bit by bit, as the man gazed into the mirror, terror burnt his expression. The hypodermic was ready.

The screen grew dark and faded as the tune switched off.

"Three hundred of them," said Scott, "just off the *Eagle*. All of them mixed up the same way, the way other ships have been since the *Wanderer*. And some of them babbling about ghostlike figures."

"What do you make of it?" asked Rafferty.

Scott snorted.

"You might as well look in Haymes' volume as anywhere else. He drew a chart to attempt to explain it. Some ships were killed off; others suffered this fate. Therefore, he reasoned, there must be a common denominator somewhere. He listed all the common articles on the ships whose passengers had suffered the fate of the *Eagle*. The list was so immense it was utterly useless. Haymes claimed that only tests with those articles used as controls would ever solve the matter. As for the ghosts, he believed in them. So do Planeteers. All I know is that when I escaped, I saw nothing. There were only sounds…terrible sounds."

"You have no faith at all in that second message?"

"We place our faith in anything until we know it is useless. It has seemed unreasonable until now to put much belief in anything so...so strange. I think about Haymes' book. It may be that if we had taken him into our confidence, he might have helped in some way. He was a prodigious worker, as his book showed. Funny about that book, the way it seems to have disappeared from bookshops. People seem to want it instinctively, wanting to read about the dangers they only *suspect* so far, not knowing really how close the danger appears to be."

"Close?" said Rafferty.

"Yes. We have an area marked off as thin ice. This morning our patrol found the *Flambeau* well out of that area, as others have been lately. The passengers were all dead, and Dr. Crane—missing! And tracing the second message, we found that it came from somewhere in the danger area. And Dr. Crane was aboard the *Flambeau* when it took off..."

"You seem to be changing your mind," Rafferty observed, quietly.

"Perhaps. I have been thinking about it for hours. It seems so meaningless...and that may well be a clue. Haymes alive, and a pirate—it doesn't make sense. But it must be investigated."

COMMANDER Scott paused on the decision and opened his snuffbox.

"You must be aware by now, Lieutenant, of the precautions we took before we decided to tell you these things. We have gone into all of your background, your personal history. We told you not because of what you knew, for that was little, but because of where it might lead you. That alone made you a dangerous man. But we try to know our men, for we ask them in these cases to carry within themselves a terrible burden. There are men among us who would not hesitate to publish the whole truth. These we fear more than any—the misguided saviors, worse than the cowardly and the mercenary. I have carried the bitter knowledge of our struggle for years. It has almost beaten me, made me into a hated ogre, a martinet whose men fear him. But it is a burden some of us must carry."

Judd Rafferty looked at his commanding officer, the cruel looking, thin little man. The inner man had been revealed. Rafferty knew then that we see each other most truly not with our eyes, but with our hearts. Sufficient understanding might transform the ugliest of men, and the lack of it blind others in the face of beauty.

Scott sat bemused, and after a while he spoke up again, matter-of-factly now.

"We are going to check on the position given in that message. Your usefulness here," he snorted, "whatever it amounted to, has just about ended. I've been thinking perhaps you would like to volunteer for active duty aboard a combat ship that will leave shortly. The mission, I hardly need say, may be fraught with great—"

"If I may, sir. Yes, sir." Rafferty didn't wait to hear the rest.

Scott permitted himself the luxury of a half smile.

"Still can't sit still, can you? You don't know how often the red field on a star has meant blood. But you'll do. And while I'm at it, perhaps it would be just as well if Lieutenant Brown, your opponent in that little argument, were also to go. I don't know how much of the record he heard, but he hasn't been inclined to talk about it. Under the circumstances, it—"

A faint *click* came from the dictascope on the Commander's desk. Scott glanced at it as if puzzled, then he rose and strode swiftly to the door. Rafferty, following, saw him run to a desk in the outer room and look at a dictascope there.

"They were connected!" Scott cried. "The film roll with us on it—every word we said—the people in the hospital—they're all on that roll and the roll is missing!"

A wind blew in from an open window. The door to the outer room was ajar. At that moment Lieutenant Brown entered. He saluted smartly.

"Lieutenant," said Scott, slowly. "You were in this room, according to my instructions?"

"Yes sir. Until half an hour ago, sir. I took the liberty of going out into the corridors for a smoke."

"Did you see anyone come in or go out of here?"

"No sir. I walked about a bit. Is anything wrong, sir?"

"No," said Scott, slowly. Only Rafferty could guess at the thoughts that were in the old officer's mind. A tiny record had vanished, and in it was enough dynamite to shatter the whole scheme of things to bits—to wake a dreaming world into a nightmare that was reality. "Nothing special at all," Scott was saying. "Nothing at all."

CHAPTER FOUR
The Invisible World

DR. Kimball Crane had been sitting hunched over in his tiny shell for a quarter of an hour when he decided that any danger from Haymes' guns was past. He had no way of knowing if Haymes had fired at all after him; his chances of escape in that event would have been one in a thousand. The probability was that Haymes hadn't wasted ammunition. Crane believed he was waiting for a slower death. And he had wanted it that way, because it had seemed to him that at least the shell offered a chance.

But when an hour had gone by, an hour in that whiteness, and he saw nothing, he wondered why he had figured on a chance. He hadn't believed the absurd story about a planet of ghosts. And yet where was he? This was no ether swirl; it was too white, too calm. Had Haymes really taken three days to bring him here? Probably not. It had been on his way, this strange phenomena that hemmed him in. And here he would die. He had done what he could. Now he could only pray that it had served some purpose.

And then he seemed to see the whiteness thinning, becoming a misty, grayish mass like smoke, and moving in streams. He knew how easy it was for a desperate man to begin imagining things, and he turned his eyes back to the control board. Haymes had assumed that Crane knew how to manage a shell, Crane thought. Possibly because he had mentioned he had been an army doctor. That had been a long time before... He was trying to keep his mind active, but it was no use. Finally he had to look out again. The smoke seemed definitely thinner!

Was he really approaching some body? He thought, suddenly, that there was a way of finding out. Turn off his power and see if he went anywhere. If there was any body about, its gravitation would pull him toward it. He moved the levers down to their resting notches.

Nothing. The shell's nose tilted down a bit, that was all. But when he looked out at the thin, convoluted forms of smoke, they were rushing past him faster than ever! That meant nothing. The smoke might really be moving, and he stationary.

But the gray was thinning out, more and more.

Brilliant—so brilliant it blinded him completely! The sudden emergence into the blaze of daylight stabbed his eyes and hit the back of his head with pain as if from a blow.

Through narrowed lids, Crane forced his eyes open and looked about.

He gasped. Perhaps five miles below, passing under the shell in panorama, was the most beautiful sight he had ever seen—a planet bathed in sunlight and reflecting its myriad colors in dazzling beauty. Was he five miles up or was this a small planet? He could not gauge one without knowing the other. But it was rushing up at an alarming pace. He reached out and flipped the power notch on under the shell. It hissed and coughed, and slowly the shell decelerated. There wasn't much more left in the compressed air cartridges, and the oxygen supply was running short.

NOW, knifing down obliquely, from his great height Crane saw cities more immense than York, more beautiful than the Interplanetary Fair City on Mars. The buildings shone in the sunlight as only whole fields of copper and brass, silver and gold and marble might shine, but in these walls there was more vibrant life and color than in any earthly materials.

And there were rivers and lakes of blue and violet and green, hills of dark emerald, plains that stretched like tabletops in mottled colors of subdued pastel shades. There was an emotional impact in the sight. Crane felt his eyes tearing, his breath coming with difficulty. He tore his eyes away as a man might who feared for his reason.

Was this the planet of ghosts? Though Crane had not the slightest idea where he was, he laughed abruptly at the idea. But where was he?

The question, he knew, would answer itself when he landed. It was becoming impossible to stay in his tiny craft. He nosed it down sharply and felt his body strain against the acceleration belt. He thought he could hear the shell singing as it dived through the atmosphere, for it was atmosphere of some sort; it had to be for any life to exist, even plant life.

The ground was looming and he burst several shots of air to slow the shell's nose. He was near a glistening white city, with many open areas in its midst, but he chose instead to land at the fringe, near the beginnings of a great plain.

Close as he was now, he saw no signs of life. There were no aerial craft anywhere in sight, no people below. Crane shuddered momentarily as he thought of ghost cities. He was straightening out for the last gliding movement, preparing to land as easily as he could.

The shell carried no landing gear of any sort, since its sole purpose was intra-spacial, but Crane managed to land it gently by alternating the fore and aft air bursts and letting it settle down. There was hardly a bump when it was over. That was that; he had landed.

And now he faced the problem of oxygen. Should he risk taking off the tightly strapped helmet? He laughed shortly. Risk it? The waste fumes were seeping back through the feed pipes. The risk lay in not taking off that helmet. The oxygen was coming through in a trickling stream that made him gasp for breath. He had to do it.

Crane slid back the cover and felt a breeze come into the shell. With a single motion he whipped off the helmet...

THE first sensation he had was that the air was perfumed with the odors of forests and living things. The atmosphere seemed hardly different from what he remembered the Earth's had been. It was dense enough, but in addition it was infinitely more fresh than any other air he had breathed in months; better than the canned air of space liners, the weighted atmospheres of other planets that imported their oxygen, or even the somewhat sickly purity of oxygen tubes. So far as Crane knew, here was the first body aside from

Earth that possessed an atmosphere fit for humans. Now he edged out of the confinement of the shell, jumped out and stretched himself. On the edge of the plain where he stood, facing the city, were fringes of trees standing in rows. They were obviously trees, but he had never seen such orderly growths. Their branches started midway up the trunk and moved upward at precise angles, like the geometric drawing of an architect. Underfoot the grass was blue-green, thick and soft, but the blades of grass seemed to be each of the same height. Together they made an unbelievably natural carpet.

In the distance he could see the rest of the city, the buildings in the background taller as they were farther away, all of them forming a stair-like arrangement that escaped the bare severity of such a plan by a skillful change in the general scheme here and there. The day was warm and balmy, and the sun, smaller but just as bright, seemed to signify midday from its position in the sky, although there was no way of knowing the length of day here. Oddly enough, there was no indication of the great masses of cloud-like white through which he had come; the sky was clear.

It was like being home again in a dream, breathing the air one loved, seeing the sun, hearing the sounds of birds. Crane stood on tiptoe and breathed deeply, and for the first time in an age, he relaxed. It hardly mattered to him that there were no sounds except of birds that he could not see, and no signs of life. Wherever he was, the face of this new world was kind and hospitable...

He saw them when they were almost upon him. There was a swarm of birdlike creatures coming down from the sky toward him. The glare of the sun had hidden them, but now these great birds were swooping straight down—directly toward Crane.

When the first one landed, Crane saw they weren't birds...

They were men with wings! But they weren't men—he had never seen such men. Now, as fully twenty of them approached and stood near him, he was awe-stricken by their perfection of face and figure. Each of them was easily ten feet tall, built almost exactly like humans, bronzed and strong, with muscular arms and legs. There was individuality in their faces, but anyone of them would have been an extremely handsome man on Earth. They seemed human, but human only in the sense of an ideal, and looking at the white, folded wings that grew from their shoulder blades, Crane held his breath. They might have come from the lore of eons past— they were godlike—stalwart, beautiful gods!

All of them wore short, gaily colored tunics and sandals, and across their foreheads were bands to match the colors of their tunics.

For a moment Kimball Crane felt a high, unreasoning elation and a madness sweep through him. He said out loud to himself, "To Heaven in a spaceship! Lord, oh Lord, where am I?" The thought struck him with a mixture of mirth and alarm, and left him chilled and quiet.

The group moved closer, towering above him. Then one of the beings said to Crane in Crane's own language.

"Where have you come from, man of Earth?"

The apparent paradox dumbfounded Crane. They seemed to know that he had come from Earth, yet they questioned him about it. They asked no further question. They stood all about him, regarding him and occasionally turning to each other in silence.

A FEW moments later, two of the winged giants flew upward. They mounted to a height of some two hundred feet, and high overhead Crane heard them call in a clear, singing voice, the same sweetly thin and musical voice in which he had been addressed. The others followed aloft, and then they were flying away, leaving him there alone!

The whole had taken a minute to happen, and beyond what he had felt, Crane had the sensation that he was somehow not important, or even a curiosity. One of them had asked a paradoxical question and they had gone. They seemed quite disinterested in him or his origins or fate.

Then, from the top of a building on the edge of the city, Crane saw a shallow, flat vessel like a saucer come floating away and toward him. It drew closer and Crane made out figures in it. The vessel flew to a position directly above him, then gently came down to settle five feet away.

There were two men in the vessel—two humans! They regarded Crane and one of them motioned him to come into the vessel. Slowly, Crane moved to them, seeing their shaven heads, their long, flowing robes of deep blue, and their eyes, lusterless and very clear and very empty—completely empty. One of them helped Crane sit down, then nodded to the other. Several score of tiny revolving blades all around the edges of the vessel began to move. The saucer ascended quickly, the blades curved inward, and the vessel began to head in the direction from which it had come.

There was something about these men that had prevented Crane from saying a word to them. They seemed to be part of the machine in which they sat. Somehow, with their half-open mouths, their intent stare into the vacant sky, they were not human, but organisms fitted into a mobile, human form for some reason.

"Hello," said Crane. He might not have uttered a sound for all the attention it got him.

Suddenly the eyes of the two creatures were fixed on something beyond Crane, something over his shoulder; the shadow lay in the vessel. Crane twisted around. Behind him, a few feet overhead, one of the winged giants hovered. His gaze was stern, more stern than Crane had imagined one of these beings could be. Crane's vessel was suddenly moving around, heading out across the plain again, as if in response to a silent command.

Like light flashing on in darkness, Crane heard—but he heard it in his mind alone, understood it, for no voice had spoken— *"Do not be afraid, man from Earth. Let the bikko take you where I have directed."*

The winged being was moving farther away now in leisurely flight. He rose higher and higher and soon disappeared from sight. What had spoken to Crane? This being high overhead? It could only have been...the only thing he could imagine it had been was—telepathy!

These creatures in the vessel with him, they had reacted as if to telepathized orders. Were they the bikko to which the winged giant had referred? And where were they now going?

THE saucer was moving over the countryside. Everywhere it looked like an idealized painting, a beautiful land in natural splendor. There were birds following them, birds with long, brilliantly colored tails, and they flew alongside like pets might after their master. But in a moment one of the two blue-clad humans in the vessel had reached out with a long pole and struck one of the birds, frightening them all away. Crane's first impulse was to stop the shaven-head. The next instant, watching the second one, Crane changed his mind. They seemed apprehensive of something. They were flying over fields of yellow grass-like growth, and the second creature had spread a large yellow cloth inside the shallow vessel, draping part of it over themselves and Crane. Some moments later, when the country underneath had changed to pale green, another cloth to match this color was substituted. They were camouflaging their vessel! Against whom? For what?

The answer could only have been that they were afraid of other winged beings, for every time they spied one in the distance, they lowered the vessel and let it hover inches above ground, stationary. There was no understanding it. And there was no one to whom he could turn.

Crane was not the sort of man on whom alarm could descend without reason. There was no cause for alarm now, but hammering in his mind was an insistent question, and other questions followed. *Where am I?* he kept saying to himself. What is this strange world of which I have never heard a single word? And what was Haymes' connection with all this, with this world unknown to men?

There was safety in asking no questions; he would only destroy himself by demanding answers. He had to remain calm... He tried to think of the vessel in which he was, of its queer composition, its two little knobs that directed it, the odd cloths and unknown fibre which covered it inside.

The cloth was changed again, this time to a deep green. Looking out over the side, Crane saw a forest underneath. They were barely swimming over the uniformly sized trees. And not far away, from the cover of the trees, a winged giant suddenly rose, glanced at their saucer, and disappeared from view again. The vessel veered sharply, turning to where the winged being had been, and when it reached the spot, it gently lowered itself to a small clearing below.

The giant was waiting there, standing on the ground. The vessel had almost touched ground when Crane heard, again in his mind alone, *"Jump."*

Crane did as he was told; he jumped from the saucer, which had not quite touched ground. The winged being came closer, scrutinized the outside of the vessel, and brushed off some scattered leaves. Evidently he was intent on leaving no trace of where this vessel had been. Then the giant transfixed the two blue-clad humans with a glance, looked at them steadily for some moments, and turned away.

The vessel rose again, paused, and moved out of view. Crane was alone with the winged giant.

"I will speak to you orally," the giant was saying. "Telepathy seems to confuse you as yet. Listen to me carefully, for there is little time."

Crane listened to the high voice speaking to him in whispers.

"You have escaped from the man Peter Haymes and your life is in jeopardy. There is almost nowhere you can hide with safety. If you are discovered, you will be driven to destruction. What were you on Earth? Open your mind to me; it will save time."

Bewildered, Crane tried to open his mind, meanwhile thinking that he hadn't the faintest idea of how to do it. Now, if it had been his mouth…

"You have merely to focus your mind on the answer," said the giant. He kept looking about him from time to time. "Fortunately, you were a doctor. I almost guessed as much from your white tunic. Now listen. Not far from here, there is a small settlement of nottars, creatures originally human and bred by we llanu for generations as hunting animals, to destroy a pestilential animal, the boranny. Remember these words and ask no questions; they must wait. You will go to this settlement and don the clothes of the last doctor, who is now dead. The search for you will begin very soon. You must remember several things. First, *you are Doctor Bell.* Second, you have been in the settlement for *four months.* Third, you must look weary and appear depressed."

The giant stopped, intent upon some sound that came faintly through the forest, a fairly distant wailing from many throats. After a moment, the winged being resumed.

"If any llanu, that is, winged men, come, try not to be near the nottars at the time. You will find a wounded one among the nottars. You must try to save it as much as possible from death. For the rest, if any llanu telepathize questions at you, remember this: we cannot read your mind unless you focus on the answer. Give only the answers to questions as to who you are, and how long you have been there, and immediately thereafter, *concentrate upon something else*, preferably your longing for Earth, and a desire to sleep. To all other questions, give no answer; concentrate on your fatigue. Your ignorance may save you, but it is best not to take the chance.

"And now, if we do not meet again, my name is Oran. Never speak to any llana unless he first gives you that name. Good fortune."

The giant made a signal for Crane to follow him, and together they moved through the forest. The wailing they had heard grew louder as they kept walking, and presently the giant stopped. Through the edges of the forest, for it came to an abrupt end not far away, Crane saw rows of low hovels, and somewhat apart from them, a hut larger than the rest. The winged being pointed to the large hut. The next moment he had turned and begun silently retracing his steps.

Crane was alone…

What was he to do? The bizarre speech to which he had listened had filled him with vague apprehension. There was no meaning in what the being had told him. And why had he told him those things? Was he defending Crane against Haymes or other…llanu? Why?

He was filled with a great indecision, and the startling instructions and strange names he had heard were ringing in his head. But Kimball Crane had long ago evolved a philosophy. Never remain idle when there is something to do; never let indecision interfere with action. Wrong action might result poorly, but it was the only way to learn. The only thing here was that it seemed possible that if Crane acted wrongly just once, he wouldn't be around to learn anything much longer.

HE was walking out of the forest, into the clearing around which the hovels were clustered. There was a throng of humans, naked except for loincloths, gathered at one end of the clearing. As he crossed into open view, that whole throng which had been wailing suddenly was stilled, and every eye followed Crane as he strode to the large hut. Crane let no curiosity stop him from following instructions. As a doctor and a soldier, he had learned to listen and obey, and he had frequently given orders which he knew his subordinates could not understand, yet he had known how vital it was that they obey exactly, unquestioningly...

But whom was he obeying? A friend? It appeared that way. But how could he be certain? What if the other winged beings had been friends, and this one, this Oran, an enemy? Then, as Crane was entering the dank, dark hovel, he laughed at himself the way he always did when he reached an impasse in his thinking. He should have demanded a written guarantee, perhaps, and if Oran was an enemy, he would hale him to court in York. That was the only recourse he would have. And laughing out loud now at the notion, Crane saw that the entrance to the hut was thick with the humans he had seen clustered at the other end of the settlement. They were regarding him intently, but none entered.

The hovel was almost entirely bare. A little light seeped in through cracks in the ceiling, which seemed covered with grass mats. Crane suddenly wondered why this was the only hut that had a roof. But then, hanging on a wall, supported by a sliver of wood, were several ragged garments of dirty white that contrasted sharply with his still clean tunic. And on the floor beside the clothes, there stood a little black bag.

He opened it.   Inside it were the tools of his trade—a doctor's instruments.

Crane turned to the door, where the crowd had grown.

"Shoo!" he shouted, making a face. He had seen by their faces that there was no one here to whom he might say, "May I have a little privacy whilst I dress?"

They scattered away, but he was about halfway through changing into the soiled clothes when they had re-gathered. They were so absolutely savage, with their sharp, white teeth, their tangled hair, their wiry, lean, deeply burnt brown bodies, that Crane forbore shouting again. It was really as if he was alone anyhow. And he was a doctor, accustomed to human bodies as much as any savage could possibly be, he smiled to himself.

The tunic into which he changed was small on him; Crane was a tall man. And furthermore, it was so soiled that his spine seemed to shiver in distaste. But it had the effect of making Crane feel somehow at home among the savages. He stepped out among them ready to embrace each one, feeling foolishly cheerful and grinning from ear to ear. A planet of ghosts indeed! It was a planet full of research possibilities.

And all at once, remembrance of a phrase of the winged being smashed into Crane's mind. He had said that these humans had been bred for generations. For generations! These were humans, not savages in the swamps of Venus, not primitive men who had degenerated in the early isolated camps on Jupiter, not beings from another world at all—but men and women like the people he had known all his life! And they had been bred for generations! How was it possible? What did it mean? The foreboding of disaster had come full-grown to him now. He stopped smiling.

THE nottars, he had to think of them by that name, were shouting to him. "Attoo—boranny—nottar." That was the way it sounded. Half of them were motioning wildly to the part of the settlement where Crane had first seen them, and half of them were motioning toward the hut. Then one of them, more ingenious than the rest, ran forward with a long stick, reached inside the hut with it, and withdrew it with the black bag dangling from the end of the stick. The nottars jumped up and down, and now all were clamoring that he follow them.

Crane saw the prostrate form of the savage before he had taken a dozen steps. Those still around him were withdrawn to give him entry. He ran the rest of the way.

There were little spurts of blood coming from the belly of the savage, coming from three neatly drilled holes there. He bent down, examined the wounds. The nottar had suffered more from fear and loss of blood than anything else. Crane was busy at once. The black bag, carried by one of the eager savages, was well stocked. He cleaned the wounds, sutured them quickly, then applied the dressings. He motioned other nottars to carry the wounded one—Crane still had no idea as to what had caused the wounds—to one of the open-roofed hovels.

And then he was treated to a strange sight. The nottars, and there were more than a hundred, men, women and children of all ages, who had gathered around Crane while he worked on the wounded man, had been intoning a sort of free-for-all chant, like a wild invocation. Upon completion of the treatment, they began to gyrate madly, leaping about in abandon, and shouting at the tops of their lusty voices. Many of them ran to Crane and momentarily kneeled before him. All in all, Crane felt that a celebration had been put on to acclaim the wounded nottar's return from certain death, and even more, to honor him. He felt somehow that there was a vast outpouring of affection, gratitude and respect for him. It moved him more deeply than he would have thought possible.

Now several nottars came running to him, bearing the bodies of small, furry animals, three-legged and three-eyed, and over each eye was a long, pointed horn. "Boranny, boranny," they shouted. Crane had his answer. This was the little animal the nottars hunted, and not without danger. And the danger explained, possibly, the necessity for a doctor to be among them.

They were skinning the animals now, and no sooner was one skinned, than its entrails were removed and the raw meat torn away and eaten on the spot by the clamoring nottars. But not before they had first offered to Crane his choice of any part of the animal, and he refused. The refusal reminded him for the first time that he was hungry, damned hungry.

It was as if thinking about it had somehow materialized an answer. Two large vessels, like the one in which he had been, had appeared from nowhere. They moved to the center of the village, hovering in mid-air some fifteen feet, and the bikko in them were throwing down food from the loaded vessels. Now there was yelling for certain. The savages ran to the vessels, scooping up as much as they could carry. And again they came to him to offer him his choice.

"Home was never like this," murmured Crane, taking a large, bright red fruit the size of a melon. He bit into it, and added, "Right!" It was as hard as a frozen potato, with as much taste as a stone might have had. He tried another fruit, long and slender and whitish, and a third, a sort of dried apricot-looking affair, and returned to the frozen potato. "Stomach ulcers in a week," he grunted, trying to chew.

HE WAS struck by the appearance of two of the nottars who were squatting near him. He could have sworn they were smiling at his distress.

Suddenly their half-smiles had vanished, and a rustle of fear and unrest swept through the settlement. The nottars paused in their eating, their faces uplifted to the sky. Crane followed their gaze and gulped. A group of llanu were flying swiftly toward the settlement!

Their immense wings blotted out the sun as they swept down, each lighting gingerly in the clearing. Many of these llanu, unlike the others Crane had seen, were old in appearance, and the edges of their wings were flecked or stained with a yellow-golden hue. They came quite close to Crane, who was even then trying to remember what Oran had told him.

"What is your name?" The question rang in an inner ear.

"Dr. Bell," said Crane aloud. He was trying to be sad, distressed.

"What is your number?" Crane looked blank.

"What number?" he asked.

"How long have you been here?"

"Four months."

He had to look weary and depressed, Crane was telling himself. But more than that, he was telling himself that he didn't like the way they were questioning him. He could almost feel their minds probing in his brain, and the look on their faces, their proud and arrogant faces, was much the same look that they bestowed on the nottars. Be careful, Crane was telling himself. This might be a matter of life and death. He was a babe in the hands of these giants, old though they might be. They were out hunting him, and he had to remember his instructions.

"How did you trim the hairs of your beard?"

The question, searching and intelligent though it was, for Crane had but a few days' growth on his face, had a side to it that seemed irrepressibly funny to Crane. It destroyed every bit of caution that Crane had gathered. He chuckled and looked at them, not knowing what to say.

"What is your number?"

That meaningless question, repeated, did the trick.

"York 12-8801," he responded. "Where can I reach you boys?"

In later minutes, Crane was to wonder why he had not been put to death at that very instant, but at the moment he was riding high. The only response to what he had said was simple. One of the llanu opened a little pouch he carried and dipped his hand into it. He came up close to Crane and scattered a blue powder over him.

Still amused, Crane watched the llanu depart, one by one. They were out of sight in a little while, flying slowly now.

His first intimation that something had gone wrong came when Crane looked about him. The nottars were scattering. Some of them were carrying babies, others nothing more precious than food, but all of them were running—running from him!

Crane rose from where he had been sitting and tried to shake the blue dust from him. It would not come off! He smashed his hand against his clothes and still it clung. What was it? Why were they fleeing?

Here and there a nottar paused to look at him, fearfully. He sensed a vast sorrow mingling with their fear. Slowly the realization came to Crane that he had been marked—singled out! For what? He looked about the almost deserted settlement, hushed as if with brooding expectancy, and felt like a condemned man. Suddenly he began to tear the clothes off—to no avail...the blue powder had gone through! It was all over his chest and arms and legs, a dye in his skin, and nothing would remove it! He ran to his bag which a nottar had thrown into the hut again, seeking for some solution which might remove the fearful stain. There was nothing in the bag that could do it…

IT WAS by then well in the afternoon. The sun had begun to cast long shadows, and twilight was descending, a beautiful twilight that was pierced by brilliant streaks of light from the setting sun as it fell over the horizon in the midst of trailing canopies of resplendent color.

Crane sat down, wearily, alone…

In the distance he seemed to see winged beings aloft. He was filled with a sense of utter desolation, and a vast loneliness came over him, a nameless fear and oppression such as he had never known. He had come through much, and now he felt it was ending. Ending soon so ingloriously, as Haymes had said, like a brief comet wasting itself. He was so far from home, on a world which had seemingly escaped detection from the great eyes of telescopes scattered through the solar system, from the constant wanderings of innumerable space voyages…or had they, like so many others, had their discoveries translated into captivity here?

He was suddenly obsessed with the notion that the world he had left behind was falling to bits, and the fragments were visible in the first few stars that had come out in the darkening sky. He had heard stories, all sorts of stories in his life. Had there been some truth to them?

There was so much he didn't know, so much that he wanted to live for. He was descending now within himself, to a world of quiet and shadow, like the world outside. He looked at the blue stains on him, and saw how they were beginning to glow with phosphorescence that would make him visible in the dark, and it brought him no further alarm. He was cold and shivering now, and memories were flooding his mind, like the memories of a drowning man. And more than ever he felt something in the air that was not placid, a gathering tension, like the ominous charge of death.

He lay on his back, trying not to remember, not to think. Worst of all was not knowing what to expect. There never was an Earth, he thought. I was born here long ago, and here I will die.

The sky had become as black as the past; the few stars were fathomless questions. From far off he heard the timid calls of nottars. The night air was filled with sweet smells that came from the woods, the smells of living things, and they seemed then to have an overwhelming fragrance, as all living things must have for men about to die.

He seemed to hear forgotten voices whispering to him in the sighing of the wind—

But there was no wind. And slowly, the voices were louder...

It broke all at once. The sounds, like tragic melodies, bringing with them the fierce terror that only the memory of terror can bring, left him cold and helpless. His muscles had ceased to respond to his demands, his body lay flexed and shaking, and the moaning that rose in the air beat over him in horrible waves.

When he saw the first of the dim forms, he knew why Haymes had called this a planet of ghosts. He saw them now, hovering, bare traceries of form, transparent and unreal. And stronger than he had seen it before was the aura that suffused them, following them as the nebulous fire of a comet's tail follows the flashing head; a golden aura that glittered like a wet veil that had been dipped in golden dust and then lit by the flickering light of a fire.

It was a maddening cacophony, the horrible orchestral music of an unplanned masterpiece, tearing at his heart and brain. The figures were wheeling faster and faster, coming lower, and the sounds had grown beyond endurance...

CHAPTER FIVE
Chlorophyll

"HERE now, sit up!" A hand was stuck in Crane's ribs, unmistakably. "Sit up and don't move!"

It was a human voice, shouting above the terrifying failing. Crane sat up. In the blue, phosphorescent light that his body gave off, he saw two—nottars! One of them had spoken to him!

"Take it easy, Doc," the nottar was yelling. "And don't be surprised at anything that happens to you. It won't last much longer."

The golden figures were whirling now at a tremendous speed, and their golden light was added to the blue. Crane forced his eyes to stay open, and he held his ears with his hands.

Suddenly one of the figures broke from the circle and shot down at the three men, seemingly passing through them. Even as it seemed to let out a great cry of pain, the others were following the first. But not all followed. That outcry, like a tortured howl that ripped at the roots of Crane's nerves, seemed to have stopped them. The last of the figures shot away with the others.

One moment chaos. The next—complete silence. The figures vanished and the sounds had stopped. The only sensation Crane had had was that his eyes had been shuttling back and forth at great speed, seemingly from several places, as if he had been moving, which he hadn't. He couldn't have moved, literally, to save his life.

Out of the feverish thoughts that ran through him, one was paramount. He was still alive. He moved one hand, then the other. He was all there.

"You all right, Doc?"

Crane was looking at the nottars. He couldn't make out anything of their faces. In the weird darkness, illumined only by that blueness, he saw only their dark, nude bodies. One of them seemed to be holding something. Crane nodded, then said.

"Are you talking to me?"

"He's all right," said the second nottar. "Let's get into that hut."

"Come on, Doc," said the first. "Shake the cramp out of your legs."

Crane followed the two nottars in the darkness. All three went into the large, roofed hut. One of the nottars began to dig in the ground, and the other went out for several moments, returning shortly.

"Still scared, Doc?"

"Who are you?" Crane had difficulty talking.

"Just a couple of educated nottars," one answered. "We went to Harvard and never got over it."

"Let the questions wait a minute, Doc," said the other. "We're too damn hungry to talk sense. Get it going yet, Steve?"

The savage whom the second had called Steve was busy with something. A tiny flame caught in a pile of brush, then grew larger, and Crane saw what was happening. They were rubbing two sticks together, making a fire in primitive fashion. There were ashes of previous fires dug up in the hut, and the charred wood that had been buried took the flames well.

"Cover up that doorway," said a nottar.

"How?" said the other. "Them damned nottars swiped the mat I took two weeks making. And they been poking holes in the roof."

"Good thing those babies came tonight. This is the first meal I won't have to gulp. There won't be a soul around after that business."

CRANE was just sitting there, listening to the conversation. The nottars were roasting boranny meat on crude spits over the fire.

"Here, Doc, try this. Isn't half-bad. We haven't had a chance to rake a fire in two nights. The nottars are watching us lately."

Crane took the meat and ate. It was tender and rather sweet, and the solid nourishment made him feel better. In the light of the fire he was looking at the two savages in the hut with him. They were the same two that he had imagined had been laughing at him. Their hunched bodies, a deeply burnt brown, and their great masses of hair threw crazy shadows on the walls of the hut. Their teeth weren't long at all. One of them was a slender person with a rather wolfish face and thick brows. The other was heavier, and his eyes gleamed humorously at Crane.

"Can't figure us out, can you, Doc?" he said, his mouth full of food. "How long you been here?"

"Didn't you get that?" said the other to the first. "I almost yelled out loud when the big boy asked him that question. The Doc said, 'Four months,' and meanwhile, plain as day, his mind is telling them. 'That's the answer I'm supposed to give instead of one day.' They nailed him easy enough after that. He wasn't thinking of the answers at all. He was thinking of what he had been told to say were the answers." He laughed.

"What got me was the way he told them his number," said the other. "His *phone* number. That'll kill 'em when it gets around. It killed me. I had to run."

"Who are you?" said Crane, quietly. They were almost through with the food.

One of the nottars wiped his mouth appreciatively. He held out a hand to Crane.

"I'm Steve. They call me Honeyboy. This is Tommy." The men shook hands all around.

"Now suppose you tell us about how you got here," said the one who had been called Tommy. "What we have to tell you can wait a while."

"You aren't nottars." said Crane. "That seems pretty plain."

"Thanks," said Steve, grinning. "No, we're not. We're here on business, and this is the only safe way to travel around here. Nice disguise, huh? Now...how about telling us your end of it."

Crane began with the hailing of the *Flambeau* and told the two everything that had happened to him. Both men listened intently to the recital saying nothing except to ask a question now and then. When Crane had finished they were quiet for several minutes.

Presently Steve said. "You're sure that message got out?"

"Almost dead certain."

"It's the first time," said Tommy. He looked to be about forty years old, and it was odd to think of him with that youthful name. He looked at his younger companion and shrugged.

"Wonder what they'll do," he said.

BOTH men were grave, preoccupied with their thoughts. They seemed to have forgotten Crane entirely for the while. When finally Steve did turn to Crane, his manner was still a bit distant.

"We don't know much, Doc," he said, "and we've been here more than ten years. But we'll tell you all of what we know. We first got here when our ship, the *Meteor II*, crashed into this planet, which is known as Amanas. It crashed because—"

"Wait a minute," said Crane. "The *Meteor II* is a biological survey ship, isn't it?"

"Was."

"That's just it. The *Meteor II* is still intact. I know because they called at the South Venus colony two years ago while I was there."

Steve regarded Tommy. "Same thing Doc Spellman said," he muttered.

"Spellman?" said Crane. "He committed suicide a year ago."

"He's still alive, a couple of hundred miles from here," said Steve. "Where did you hear that?"

"They told me Spellman had gone crazy with the heat in Mercury," said Crane, "and swallowed acid."

"He was aboard the *Raven,*" said Tommy, "when Haymes took off the passengers and sold those who were still alive down the river."

"I never heard a word about the *Raven* going under," cried Crane.

"What's the use?" said Steve. "I told you we don't know much. The only thing we figured out was that nobody on Earth seems to know what's been going on. They're keeping the whole thing quiet, and it staggers my imagination to think about how they've managed to do it. Tommy and I are colonists ourselves, from Church's planet. We've been hearing stories since we were kids. At least we suspected."

"Where were you?" Crane broke the silence.

"Yeh. Well, the *Meteor II* crashed because the whole crew was wiped out. Tommy and I were in the laboratory when the Raie—that's what they call those babies who came to visit you about an hour ago—when they went through the ship.

That's what saved us, along with one or two others who aren't around anymore. When we saw the ship diving out of control we made a rush for the crash chambers. And we lived through it. Haymes wasn't around yet in those days. The llanu took us off and got us to work on their shrubbery. Then they found out we were suspecting too much and they got the notion we would be better off as bikko—the boys in the blue bathrobes. Know what's wrong with them? *They're decerebrated!* The *llanu* take out most of their brains, and then they move them around by telepathy! A real nice business, isn't it?

"Well, Tommy and I couldn't see ourselves in blue, so we beat it. We knew enough by then to know that the worst the llanu could do to us, and we took the chance. Listen, Dr. Crane—"

"How do you know my name?"

"Ah, everybody knows it by now. Your mind was yelling it at those llanu when you said 'Dr. Bell.' Tommy and I have picked up a few things around here in our time. We listened in on that questioning..."

A BRIEF silence fell over the men, and they sat gazing into the last embers of the fire, none of them thinking of anything in particular, and yet all of them quieted somehow.

"Dr. Crane, do you know how many humans there are on this planet?" said Steve. "Maybe ten thousand, in one form or another. They've been taking them off ships for almost two hundred years. They've got them hunting animals, as nottars, and cultivating undersea fungi for food, as spregg, and they use them as personal servants, as bikko. Some have more brains than others. And there are a handful of men like us, still sound in mind and body, because they need them, because they have to have them around to take care of the nottars and the spregg. And because the rebels among the llanu are anxious to have normal men on Amanas."

"Rebels?" said Crane.

"Like that Oran," said Tommy. "There are maybe a thousand of them. They're the most religious race you ever heard of—and the most bloodthirsty, when you look at what they want objectively."

"What do they want?"

"The Earth!"

"What for?"

"I don't know. They're ready to knock off every living being on Earth. Their word for Earth is Poros. It means 'End of Sorrow.' It's tied up with their religion in some way. The rebels are heathens, and they are against the plan of the priests. But they don't have anything to do with us because we killed a couple of llanu once by accident. Death is the worst thing that can happen to them. They're forbidden to kill anything at all. That's why they use nottars to hunt for them; they can't even kill the boranny."

"But they do kill," said Crane. "I saw them do it. They might have killed me tonight if you hadn't saved me. I still don't know how."

"They don't kill," said Steve. "The Raie do it. It isn't the same thing. And when you've got something to stop the Raie, they can't touch you outside of trying to get the bikko to heave you off a high place or something, and the bikko are the lousiest fighters you ever saw. Before Haymes came into the picture there wasn't a thing the llanu could do. Now Haymes comes after us from time to time with heat guns."

"Heat guns!" said Crane suddenly. "I've got one!" He jumped up and ran through his tunic, still hanging on the wall.

"Don't bother looking," said Steve. "Oran probably took it away without your knowing it. There are no weapons on

Amanas except the ones Haymes and his men tote. The llanu are afraid they might be used on them, but they seem to let Haymes carry them, maybe because they can't stop him."

Crane found nothing in his tunic. Confused, he sat down again.

"What has Haymes got to do with all this?" he said.

"We thought at first that he had made some kind of a bargain with them, that he was acting like a slave trader. Then when we found out what had happened to him on Earth, and the way he disappeared and showed up here, we didn't know what to think. From things we hear from time to time, like the stuff you told us, it seems he's working with them for another reason, maybe as a partner. They don't like him much. When he goes out among them, he has a bodyguard of twenty men. But since he appeared, the ships that have disappeared have mounted by the threes."

"What does it all mean?" said Crane, slowly.

"It means," Steve answered, his finger drawing a line across the ground, "that pretty soon there won't be that old place we used to call home. Tommy and I have been fighting from undercover for years, and where has it gotten us? If Haymes hadn't come, maybe we would have organized a decent revolution here. We're still trying."

"How?" said Crane.

"YOU haven't been here long enough," said Steve. "You haven't seen the way other normal humans appear after awhile. They're the sorriest creatures on Earth—on Amanas. They're desolate, they're lonely, they're filled with a strange sadness—the way that Oran told you to act. That would have been normal for a doctor here four months. When they don't kill themselves, they go crazy."

"Tell him the rest in a hurry," said Tommy. "We haven't much time."

"Time for what?" said Steve. "We aren't going any place." He chuckled disconsolately. "That's the way they all sound, Doc. It's getting me now a little. You know what it is? These llanu have whisperers among them. They are a special group whose function it is to fly around where there are normal people, humans, and whisper to them. You had a taste of it, I think, when you were out there alone a while back. You don't even know there's anyone telling you things, making you think the things you're thinking. They take the spirit out of a man. Take away a man's will to fight and what have you got? That's a refinement of telepathy that's got hypnotism whipped to a standstill.

"That's where we come in. Tommy and I do pretty well in the telepathic business. It's mostly a language of symbols. Our language isn't easy for llanu to get, but with their brains, when they do get it, they're damned good at it. But they can't read your mind if you won't focus on what they're after. Tommy and I let our hair grow and we act like nottars or like spregg, or even once, like bikko. The language of the primitive humans—they've bred 'em long enough—doesn't have more than two dozen words, and when we think in those words, they can't tell us apart.

"So that's what we do. We go around from place to place undoing the work of the whisperers, educating the normal humans, and showing them how to get away from the Raie."

"How did you save me?"

"We held on to one of these lilacs."

"What?" Crane looked at an Earthly lilac plant that Tommy took from one of the darkened corners of the hut. "You're not kidding?"

"No." Steve's expression changed from one of half-hearted banter to an earnestness that was almost sad to see. "It's all we have and it isn't much. You see, Tommy and I were playing with this plant, or its great-great-great grandfather, when the *Meteor II* went down. It saved us."

"It doesn't make sense."

"Yes it does." Tommy shook his head with a half-smile of sympathy. It was strange to see these men smile. They looked like savages, crouching low in a red and blue darkness, hardly able to see each other. "Did you notice any of the leaves on the trees when you came here?" Did you see that greenish light that Haymes played on the Raie? That's the answer. Doctor, *there is no chlorophyll on this planet.*"

When they thought that the words had made their impression, Steve took up the conversation. "All the trees and plants that you see on this planet are not real! They're synthetic...in a way. Oh, they're real enough in most ways. They grow, they reproduce, they have seeds—but even the seeds have to be nursed. Their plants don't have chlorophyll."

"Plants can't live without chlorophyll," observed Crane.

"Not so," Steve said. "These llanu have succeeded, I am certain, in finding another source of energy than sunlight. They synthesize the food they feed these plants with that energy, perhaps atomic energy. They have colored their plants with internal pigments so that again they resemble earthly plants, although chlorophyll, which has a green pigment, is entirely missing."

AS STEVE paused, Crane waited a moment. It was so strange to hear him speaking in formal language after listening to his colonist's slangy way of expressing himself. Probably the years here had also had their share in submerging the scientist within Steve. He had not even given another name. Just Steve.

"Wrong again, Doc." Steve smiled. "You forget I know what's going on in that head of yours. I haven't been submerged. I am like a swimmer in an impossible sea, content to float awhile until I see something to swim to. What took me only a minute to tell you, I was years in finding out. And I still don't know why the llanu have done all this. It isn't reasonable. But maybe when I know that, I'll know everything.

"There's just this left to tell. Chlorophyll, a completely extraneous substance here, nothing more than a complex ester with the physical properties of lipins, soluble in ether or alcohol but not in water, formed of carbon, hydrogen, oxygen, nitrogen and magnesium—is a poisonous substance to the Raie!

"Don't ask me why. I don't know. I don't know what the Raie are. I think they're some sort of half-alive substance, a stabilized energy form of a kind, and chlorophyll tends to destroy their balance. They seem to have a consciousness. Haymes can direct them. The priests, I have heard, can communicate with them. But when they come near chlorophyll..."

"Yes?" said Crane, suddenly tense.

"Something peculiar happens. Ordinarily the Raie kill humans. But when they come near chlorophyll, something strange happens. They seem to be able to—how can I tell you this—to take out the essence of a human being, his personality, his 'I am,' and exchange it for another. If there is no other human about, that cannot happen."

"But why didn't—" Crane began.

"It did. It happened before outside. It happened so fast you didn't even know it. Remember when you seemed to be looking on from several different places at once? You were, actually. The fortunate thing was that this time, the switches came out all right in the end. Tommy and I were a little afraid, in advance, thinking about how you might have reacted if the switch hadn't been completed. Tommy and I have been switched for weeks on end sometimes. We seem to get along in each other's bodies, though, don't we, Tommy?"

Tommy smiled.

"I'm going to chop off one of your arms next time I'm you," he said. "You eat too fast for me."

Crane couldn't believe what he heard. It sounded so—

"Yeh, it's crazy," Steve agreed. "Once I was in the body of some half-gone bikko in the brass city. That was a close call. I'll tell you about it sometime…if we're all still around…"

"The way you joke about it." It was all Crane could say.

"You're quite a joker, yourself," said Tommy. "Maybe that's why we three are alive after what's happened to us. I have a theory—"

"SAVE it," Steve interrupted, grinning. "The thing is, as long as we can joke, we know we're safe from the whisperers, at least. And it saves our courage. We have a lot of work here. I have a little laboratory fixed up a long way from here, and in between our road trips of keeping up the local morale, I work on the lilacs to build up our supply of chlorophyll. We grow them and give the seeds away, making more and more lilacs. Once, three years ago, we had a little city of our own, completely surrounded by lilacs. They had to get Haymes to come and tear it down. That's when he found out about us."

"What probably saved me on the *Flambeau*," Crane mused aloud, "was that I was playing around with the Venusian swamp fever serum when the Raie broke out. It was the chlorophyll, and not Haymes that spared me. But I can't figure out why he didn't just kill me on the *Flambeau* when he came back. Was I a good audience?"

"Bothers me too," said Tommy.

"Probably bothers Haymes more than any of us," said Steve.

Crane started to fill in the details of what had happened on Haymes' ship when Tommy interrupted.

"Save it, Doc," he said. "We can see everything in your mind before you even say it. We know all about it. Haymes pulled you off the *Flambeau* and into his ship. You irritated the hell out of him. Took a lot of courage saying the things you said to him." Tommy smiled. "Then again it might have just been stupidity on your part. Then you saw Haymes stab the Raie with the green ray from that silver tube. Wish you could have gotten away with one of those things. Steve and I would love to break one open and examine it. It seems to give Haymes a certain control over the Raie. We're trying to do the same thing in Steve's laboratory. We've been working on it for two years."

"And when we get it," said Steve, lying down and yawning, "then we'll make a spaceship out of a couple of trees and beat it out of here."

"That's as good a note as any to go to sleep on," said Tommy, stretching out near Steve. "There's a big day ahead of us tomorrow. We're going hunting in the forest. That's why we're here now." He mumbled something about explaining better in the morning. Then he grunted. "Doc, will you turn off that blue light? It's going to keep me awake all night."

Crane looked at the phosphorescent glow on him and laughed.

"It'll go away in a couple of days," said Steve, sleepily. "And don't worry. We're safe enough here as long as Haymes' lads don't come, and the lilacs keep doing their share. So go to sleep."

Crane slowly laid down, his brain still restive, tired as he was. What a day it had been! How much beyond his imagination...

Here he was, alone on a distant planet, an unknown planet, with two men who had been strangers to him some short hours before. Now they were the closest kin he possessed. There was some comfort in the company of two brave and intelligent men. Crane never thought of himself as either brave or intelligent. He just went along, the way he had all his life, being a doctor or a soldier or an extra hand at a dice game, living the way he thought a man should live and not bothering to mull about it too much.

In that way he was more like his two new companions than he realized, but the realization was not lost on them.

He remembered again Haymes' words about the comet wasting itself. He had been wrong. There was more than one comet, there were many more. And if there were enough, perhaps... "You have fallen into the orbit of a plan," Haymes had said. Comets had more than once destroyed plans and orbits, when they met...

It was very quiet outside now and Crane was tired out. He knew he would fall asleep soon, and he was a little afraid of it.

The Raie.

He was afraid to close his eyes for long. But he had to try.

"Listen, Doc," Steve's voice yawned to him. "You been keeping that head of yours going so fast that I got to like it. It rocks me to sleep. So don't stop now, or I won't be able to stand it. Here's something to chew on: these llanu are a pretty healthy race; they live to the ripe old age of two thousand years. They'll be around a lot longer than you or Tommy or me. Try that on your merry-go-round."

Crane was wide-awake again for the next quarter hour, wondering.

And not until he heard Steve snoring peacefully was his mental meandering halted. He closed his eyes.

CHAPTER SIX
The Message from the Grave

CRANE was startled to awakeness, instantly alert. Standing over him were Steve and Tommy. It took a moment before Crane even remembered who they were, the cobwebs of sleep momentarily blurring his memory. Over their shoulders, from where they stood in the doorway, the first yellow rays of the sun were slanting down cheerfully.

"Nice work," Tommy said to Steve. Both were grinning. Tommy said to Crane, "Come on with us. The nottars are coming back.

Crane shook the sleep that was still pulling at him out of his eyes. His bones ached when he got to his feet, and he groaned audibly.

"Don't either of you two believe in nice long dreams?" he scowled.

"Let's get going," said Steve. The three moved out of the hut and into the clearing where the low hovels in their dark circle stood all around them. Here and there a nottar walked about, stretching, and pausing the instant he spied the three men to look at them attentively. "Into the forest primeval we go," said Steve.

"Into the forest phony, you mean," said Tommy.

"Phony or not," said Steve, "we've got to find it today, even if we have to kill a nottar to do it. We've been here three days already, and if we stay any longer, some wandering llanu may take a peep into the dark blanks that these nottars have for minds, and they'll see some of that slow, growing suspicion that they're eyeing us with."

Every nottar that was about was looking at them as they left the settlement and were swallowed up in the woods.

"See that one over there?" said Tommy. "He's thinking that it's funny we go out hunting early every morning, stay out all day, and come back at night to mooch boranny meat from the others. He doesn't think we're much good."

"He thinks the Doc is good, though," said Steve.

"What do you mean?" Crane asked.

"When I tuned in to his mind he was puzzling over the fact that you're still alive, Doc," Steve answered. "Just let some llanu tune in on that. They'll call out Haymes' boys."

The three men were walking deeper into the forest, saying nothing. Crane looked about at the trees in an endeavor to see how they differed from Earthly or interplanetary trees. Outside of a preponderance of seemingly prehistoric specimens—the kind that were found petrified on Earth—he could see no difference. He even identified what he thought was an oak.

"You said something to me when you first woke up," said Steve, conversationally, "something about me believing in nice long dreams. The answer is, I do. Especially when I've made 'em. Didn't you have a dream about a four-headed dragon with spaceships for teeth about to take a bite out of you?"

Walking alongside, Crane nodded.

"Well...that was me," said Steve. "Tommy and I play like that. That's the way we wake each other up. First one up whispers a dream into the other's ear. I got Tommy this morning—and then you. Did you like it?"

"You mean you telepathized a dream to me while I was asleep?" said Crane.

"Yeah," Tommy chuckled. "Or else you'd still be sleeping. I tell you this telepathy business has more angles..."

Steve smiled meagerly. "We'd knock 'em dead back home…"

THEY had walked a bit further when Tommy pointed to a spot ahead where three huge trees stood close together.

"About here, I think," he said. Steve nodded and turned to Crane.

"Doc," he said. "We're going to hunt for something. I'll outline it briefly. The guy ahead of you in that settlement, Doc Bell, was supposed to be a queer egg. He got more information out of the rebel llanu than any of us. We got word a few weeks ago that he had eavesdropped on a conversation that gave him a clue to escaping from this planet. A traveler like us, named Abe, found out about that conversation and he told us me it.

"It seems Doc Bell was up before the Tribunal of the llanu, and they questioned him."

"The Tribunal?" Crane asked.

"Huge place—big as a city. Filled with llanu and captive humans. There's a big chamber there where humans are brought before the Tribunal council and judged. Abe was there posing as a bikko and he and the Doc got together for a few moments before the Tribunal came into session. The Tribunal turned Bell over to Haymes, but Abe got away somehow. He said the Doc was part of the 'Chain'—at least that's what the Doc told him—and the Chain was buried in the nottar's holy graveyard."

"What do you mean—Chain?" Crane asked.

"Just think your questions to me," said Steve. "I'll get to them all. The Chain is a series of documents…usually written on cloth…that are bundled together and hidden in the graveyard. It's a system that's been going on for many years, almost exclusively among the doctors. Tradition says that whenever a doctor has found out important information regarding the llanu or Amanas, and which he wants to pass on to his successor when his time is up, he writes it down and leaves it in the nottar's graveyard. Any doctor who has been around for any length of time is eventually taken to the graveyard by the nottars. Whenever a nottar is accidentally killed by the Raie, his fellow nottars bury him in this secret place—it's very holy to them. Not even a llana can get a nottar to show them where the location is, and if anybody tries following them, the nottars simply stay away from it.

"Over the years, the doctors came to realize that they were the only outsiders trusted by the nottars, and because of this trust they were allowed into the graveyard, usually as part of the burial ceremonies. So as time went by, it hit upon them to begin hiding information in the graveyard, where it would be safe from all prying eyes. That's how the Chain was born. And each time a doctor added something to it, he would number it—always one number higher than the previous doctor. They never used their names, only numbers."

"Clever," Crane observed. "It kept their identities secret in the event the Chain was found by the llanu."

"That's right," Steve continued. "The Chain has been around for a long time. It has all kinds of vital information in it—things about telepathy and the whisperers, and how to fight them...all kinds of stuff."

"Did the llanu ever find out what the doctors were doing...about the chain?" Crane asked.

"Yeah," said Steve. "And by using their telepathic powers, they'd try to catch them off guard and then shoot them questions. They'd ask, like they asked you yesterday, 'What number are you?' Usually, before the Doc could think better of it, he'd have focused on the answer, if he knew it. I don't know what number you are, but if there were five ahead of you, then you'd be number six. And the only way you could ever know what number you were was if you had added something to the Chain. The llanu fear the Chain because of the information it holds. They've been trying to find it for years."

"That's part of the reason we need to find it first," Tommy added.

Steve continued, "Anyway, they pulled in Doc Bell and put him up before the Tribunal after he slipped up and gave out his number. Fortunately, Abe was there and got a lot of info out of the Doc before his hearing. He passed it all on to me. Doc Bell's part of the Chain mentions a possible way of escape from this planet—that's the main reason we're looking for it. He also told us the nottar's graveyard is marked by a flat black slab of stone.

"That's the landmark we're hunting for. We've been all through this forest up to about here. We're going to scatter now and continue searching. Every minute counts. So let's scatter now. Keep in touch and keep your eyes open. We don't fully know what Abe's information may mean." His voice fell. "We don't know whether this is the solution to our imprisonment on this planet or not. But it may well be. And there's something in here..." He tapped his chest. "...that says it is."

THAT same something was also beating wildly in Crane's chest when they moved apart. Underneath the bantering tone that Steve had used he had also heard an undercurrent of deadly seriousness. These two, Tommy and Steve, had put their lives at risk by coming into the forest in search of the nottar graveyard.

Every moment was fraught with the fear of discovery by the llanu. A tiny oversight would lose, perhaps forever, the clues that these men had been gathering for years, trying to find salvation. It was salvation not for those who had recorded the information through the years, but for those others who as yet knew nothing of this hidden world of the llanu—those who knew nothing of the fate that lay in store for them. It was a fate that Crane considered with much trepidation.

Tommy had implied that Earth's future was at stake. It was too huge a concept to swallow all at once. Suddenly Crane remembered another of Haymes' phrases, when he had said: "…we are not the freebooters of another age. Our prize is an exceptional one…" The fate of a world in so few hands…the hand of men.

From time to time he kept calling out, keeping within sound of both his companions. They were going deeper into the forest, combing it with care, each man's eyes intent on what lay about him.

The sun had mounted high in the heavens when they met again. There was a drinking well and they gathered around it. The well was one frequented by nottar huntsmen.

"We'll have to move faster. The place is getting filled with those nottar savages; I heard a few earlier," said Tommy. His lean face was perspiring, and his cheekbones glistened darkly where a stray ray of sunlight came through the trees to play about his head.

Crane drank his fill. "Is this where the nottars hunt the boranny? If it is…" he paused, looking around, "I haven't seen any at all."

"That's because you haven't been bred for a century to see them," said Steve, ruefully. "Let's get moving again."

An hour later, Crane let out a yell.

"You shouldn't have shouted so loud," said Steve, his eyes opening wide, staring down at a flat black stone that was covered over with uprooted vegetation. It was perhaps fifteen feet square, and some three inches thick. "If the nottars come across us now…" He left the sentence unfinished as he gazed intently at the black stone.

They began pushing away at one corner of the stone, trying to move enough of it to allow one man to squeeze through. Slowly the backbreaking work paid off. The slab moved away inch by inch, revealing the pit that it covered. They struggled with it until there was a hole about two feet wide.

Without pausing for breath, Tommy lowered himself feet first into the pit. They heard him land heavily below. The stench of decaying bodies rushed through the opening, foul and revolting, but neither Crane nor Steve budged from the opening.

Steve murmured, "You brought us luck, Doc."

"Happy to help," Crane responded.

The pair waited many minutes for Tommy to return. Neither spoke. Finally they heard a voice from below.

"Got it."

Steve lowered his legs through the opening for Tommy to grab onto, Crane holding on to him. They had Tommy out of the pit a few moments later. In his hand he was holding a rolled bundle of cloth. He sat down on the slab and began unrolling it. There were tiny crude letters written all over what had once been a surgeon's tunic.

"Written in blood," said Crane.

The letters were a faded brown.

Tommy kept unrolling the bundle. It was many garments and pieces of cloth bundled together. His eyes scanned over the many crude writings.

"A lot of this appears to be routine medical stuff," he said, pointing. Steve looked in and read, too.

"But this—from here on…"

THEY commenced to reading what appeared to be an important section. Tommy kept shaking his head, saying, "What does he mean about the connection of the llanu and the Raie. And this about Amanas starting to move closer to the solar system about two hundred years ago?"

Steve didn't know. All he said to Crane was, "You're number 24 in a long line of brilliant men, Doc."

Twenty-four. Through the years they had compiled their vague encyclopedia, passing it on from man to man, fighting alone on a strange world, hoping to leave valuable information for others in the future. Crane felt like he was hearing voices from the grave.

"Lord!" Steve whispered forcefully. His face looked almost grayish, his eyes bloodshot. He pointed down at what he'd been reading. "According to Doc Bell's section they're moving closer to Earth every day, and there aren't many days left..." He looked down and started reading again. "The deserted white city...a ship made of gold...in the pit..." He was mumbling as he read.

Tommy began rolling up the bundle of cloth while Steve was still reading.

"We've got all the information we need right here," Steve said, looking up at Tommy. "I'll take the Doc and make for the white city. According to what I've just read, our means of escape lies there. If there's a way off this planet, that's where we'll find it. You go for Harvey, Tommy. We'll all rendezvous in three days—that ought to be enough time."

"Wait a minute, who's Harvey?" asked Crane.

"One of us," Steve answered. "A friend of ours, and he's in the hands of the llanu right now."

Crane seemed almost peeved at hearing this. "Well thanks for telling me..."

Tommy put his hand on Crane's shoulder. "Didn't want to worry you with a lot of extra details, Doc. But we've got to get him back before he's decerebrated."

"Decerebrated...like the bikko?"

"Yeah, Doc," Tommy answered, "like the bikko."

"How did the llanu get their hands on him?"

"It's a long story," Steve answered. "We found out he'd been taken by the llanu right before we found you. I'll tell you more on the way. Right now we've gotta get moving."

"Put the bundle back inside the pit," said Tommy, grimly. "There's a chance we could get captured and we wouldn't want it to fall into the wrong hands…"

Steve held out a restraining hand. "Never mind," he said. "If we're killed or captured by the llanu it won't make any difference. There probably won't be another doctor down the line to read it. Besides, we may need to refer back to some of the information contained in these writings. You keep the Chain for the time being, Tommy. There's a lot of info about the inside of the Tribunal—you may need it."

Suddenly there was a swooshing noise from behind. The next instant the three of them wheeled around. Crane let out a gasp…

All three were facing a llana!

The winged giant towered over them, holding out a hand.

"Give it to me," he said, orally. "This is forbidden."

Steve took a deep breath and answered, "Not on your life. If you try to take it away from us we'll fight to the death. Chances are you'll end up killing at least one of us. Even if you are a llanu rebel, that's still taboo."

Tommy, acting as cool and calm as possible, said, "We should get going now."

At that the llana made some odd motions toward his wings.

Steve said, "What's he doing?"

Crane looked closely at the llana, it was Oran, the winged rebel who had first befriended him. As Oran looked out into the forest, his brow clouded, and his hands were tightly holding the edges of his immense white wings.

"Calling the nottars—that's what he's doing!" Tommy cried.

The llana looked at Crane.

"I helped you. I tried to save your life. Is this the way you repay me? You must be patient, and go the way of peace. Oran is your friend."

"Talk to his lawyer," said Steve sarcastically between his teeth. "You rebels are a lot of talk. Patience? What will you do for us after Haymes gets a hold of us and…" He paused for a moment, then looked at his companions. "…let's get the hell out of here."

Steve led the way. Crane and Tommy followed, running after him at a fast lope. And from behind them, from Oran, each man heard in his mind the words, *"Your action may result in the death of every man on Amanas."*

"He knows what we've found out," Tommy panted. "Now we're really in for it."

"We've got to get Harvey before then," Steve answered as he ran.

"How?" Crane gasped.

"About an hour from now…when the ses come…we'll need two of them."

"What in the world is a ses?" Crane asked, a puzzled look on his face.

"They're the saucer-shaped hovercrafts you saw earlier, the ones manned by the bikko," Steve answered. "Getting a couple of them is part of our plan."

Tommy suddenly stopped dead in his tracks. Half a dozen nottars directly ahead were running sullenly toward them. Tommy slipped a hand under his loincloth, to where a little bag hung strapped to his naked back. He opened the bag and dipped his hand in. The first nottar to approach them got a handful of blue powder right in his eyes. The second had his face smeared with it by Tommy. The third ducked and howled. In a moment they were all shrieking as they saw the blue powder on two of their companions.

The three men were running again. No one came near them...

THE settlement was deserted when they returned. In the distance the whole forest was ringing with the terrified crying of the nottars. In front of one hut were several dead boranny, untouched.

"Bad news travels fast even here," Tommy grunted. "Doc, you get that black bag of yours. It might come in handy. And lend me a knife or a scalpel or something. I'll skin these boranny while we're waiting."

"Waiting for what," Crane asked.

"Be patient," said Steve. "You'll find out soon enough."

Crane brought out the black bag and watched Tommy expertly skin the dead boranny. Crane could feel the tension creeping up his spine. Every moment they sat there was like sitting on the edge of a volcano about to erupt. Would Haymes' men be sent out to hunt them down?

"One question at a time, Doc," said Tommy, reading Crane's thoughts. He peeled off a layer of boranny skin. "Now what's that big question about the chlorophyll that's been eating you?"

Crane grinned. "It isn't safe with you two around peering into my mind all the time. I'm glad now I led such a clean life. About the chlorophyll, I've been wondering why, if it indeed poisons the Raie, how they can possibly do any harm on Earth."

"That's a good point, Doc...but how much chlorophyll do you think there is in a city like York?" Steve countered. "And maybe there are other weapons at the llanu's disposal we know nothing about."

"You know," said Tommy, "they plan on moving against Earth pretty soon. I figure in another week or two at the outside."

Crane then looked up and saw what they had been waiting patiently for. The ses saucers laden with food for the nottars were descending over the center of the settlement. The bikko in them were leaning over the sides, throwing the food down from their perch ten feet over the ground.

"Look at them," said Steve sourly. "Wasting that perfectly awful food, without giving a damn whether there's anyone around to eat it."

"Which of those ses should we go for?" asked Tommy.

Steve pointed a finger at a vessel manned by two bikko, hovering near them. Both men darted toward the hovercraft. Steve clasped his hands, forming a step. Tommy lifted a naked foot into the step, Steve heaved up, and Tommy shot up into the air, grasping one end of the vessel. Before he could climb over the edge he was seen. One of the bikko swung over and began to hammer his hands. The other calmly began to manipulate the machine. The vessel started to spin, faster and faster. Tommy's body was lifting up horizontally from the centrifugal force, but he refused to let go. The vessel was not only spinning. It was moving along over the huts. Steve looked on helplessly, then followed Crane, who was climbing up on the roof of a hovel. The vessel was quickly coming near it.

The bikko saw too late the two men on the roof. Crane broad-jumped right into the center of the craft. He reached out for the throat of the bikko flying the ses, got it, and held on until the vessel stopped spinning. Then he swung around and smashed his fist into the other's face. The bikko spun around and fell out of the vessel, hit the roof, rolled down, hit the ground, got up, fell down dizzily, got up again and began running.

And then Crane was laughing. Steve was leaning over the side, playfully pummeling Tommy as he tried to climb up. Then all three of them were laughing.

CRANE looked around. The other vessels were still calmly discharging their food as if nothing had happened.

"How's that for discipline?" said Steve. "Once they get orders, they stick to 'em. The only departure is in an emergency, like when someone tries to take their ses away. Nice trick."

Tommy was playing with the knobs that controlled the vessel. The ses began to move closer to the others.

"You know I don't know how Steve and I got along without you, Doc."

"Thanks," said Crane. "I like you boys too."

Tommy moved the vessel alongside another ses. Crane stood up and carefully stepped over. He held the bikko by the collar of his robe for a moment, hit him, and sat him down. The saucer was starting to spin, but Crane reached out, grabbed the other bikko, jabbed his left arm forward. Then Steve crossed over.

"Ever do any amateur boxing?" he asked, working the controls to ease the vessel to the ground.

"A little, in the army," said Crane. He helped Steve roll out the bodies of the still-dazed bikkos. They rose their craft up next to Tommy's.

Tommy called out to them, "Remember the plan. You two are off to the white city. I'm going to locate Harvey." Tommy held out his hand toward the other ses. "This may be goodbye," he was saying. He had a grin on his face, but somehow it was crooked and his voice had a huskiness in it.

"So long," said Steve, shaking Tommy's hand. "Be careful."

"See you soon, Tommy…" said Crane. "…see you soon." His eyes were glistening and he felt choked up inside.

"Three days," said Tommy, turning away. "June 11th."

As the two vessels began to separate, Steve yelled, "See if you can find a couple of girls for me and Doc, will you?"

Tommy made a face and answered, but he was too far away to be heard.

The little saucer-like ships were drawing farther and farther apart. In a while, they were out of sight of each other.

CHAPTER SEVEN
The Mission of the Solitary C

JUNE 11, 2770 was a day long remembered.

It was a Monday, and that in part accounted for the way in which the avalanche started, for people of all nations had gone peacefully out to their daily tasks early in the morning, and that at first kept them from hearing everything all at once. But the avalanche, slow to start, became impossible to stop once it had begun.

It came roaring down suddenly, all at once—the reckoning of two centuries, long overdue, claiming its own…

The day had come, bringing with it a bleak, cold rain and an unseasonal chill. Millions who might otherwise have been outdoors were confined to their homes, and that was another factor.

At first, people were inclined to regard what came over their Audipress attachments to the visiscopes as entertainment. In bad taste, of course, and rather juvenile thriller entertainment…and disconcerting. But little by little, as it continued, the first few calls that went to Audipress headquarters were unanswered. That was a mistake. People began to call friends, and the friends called others.

The really alarming feature of the broadcast came when it ended. Then, instead of one of the personable staff of Audipress showing his face on the screen, the screen went blank. And a voice, just a voice, without any face at all, said things no one should have said:

"What you have just seen and heard is not a fabricated teleplay. This is a 'stolen' record of actual facts regarding an impending danger to Earth. It is not coming to you via Audipress. We are blocking the regular channels of Audipress to show to the citizens of America and the world the appalling news that has been kept from them. You have only to dial the press outlet nearest you for confirmation."

That was all, at first. It should have been obvious to those who did call that no news agency could have handled so many calls all at once. And then there was a short flash on the visiscope screens and they lit up again, and suddenly there was the familiar face of a newscaster. He asked for a discontinuation of the calls, smiled at the people's alarm over what was a "harmless experimental story," and began to report the news of the day.

But at that moment his image faded.

The screen blanked out completely. The voice that had spoken before was heard once again. It had a chilling effect.

"We have cut in again, and we will continue to block the regular Audipress wavelength as long as our whereabouts remain undiscovered by the authorities. There is a human duty to perform. Courageous men have undertaken that work all over the world, simultaneously, from many hidden stations. Look at the screen. You cannot any longer doubt the authenticity of the recording. These are no actors. *Demand to know the full truth…*"

The broadcast that had first been aired was repeated. It brought out two facts. First, that it was a recording of some sort being broadcast. Second, there was no doubt that the screen was showing people who were not actors. By some horrible twist of irony, Commander Scott, out of the many men whom it might have been, was the central figure in the broadcast...

IT WAS not a play. It was true, all of it. And people were all the while calling others, or calling Audipress and getting no response. Those who had high-powered sets tuned in other continents and got the same thing in many languages.

Things were being broadcast about duplicates of ships...people missing...insurance claims—and Commander Scott was saying them, caught on some secret camera, saying them all to a strong-faced, earnest young man, Judd Rafferty, because it had been found politically necessary to tell him. Him, and so few others, the wearers of the red field!

"The day they find out will be a sad day indeed..."

Scott had said that, his gloved hands playing with a snuffbox.

And the hospital, and all those people in it, the doctors, the talk of Haymes, long-forgotten Haymes, the *Flambeau*, and the danger, the danger that was coming closer and closer to Earth—and no one knew what it was. "How really close the danger appears to be..." and the part where Scott said, "...these we fear more than any, the misguided saviors..."

A voice then broke in to say, "*We* are the misguided saviors, the men who have not hesitated to publish the whole truth, telling our fellow men of things shrouded in secrecy, demanding the end of involuntary sacrifice."

It kept up that way all afternoon, with the recording going on over and over and over, and the voice growing louder. And all over the world a fear-stricken humanity poured forth from its work, to stand and look at the heavens and wonder. Night or day, it made little difference. There was terror in the depths of the sky, and where people had been asleep, there was no more sleep. People were calling, calling, calling—and getting no answers. This was slowly driving the populace crazy. And then the whole southwest section of America stopped getting the recording right in the middle of the broadcast, with not a word from Audipress, not a word, even of denial...

One by one the broadcasts were being blacked out. There were people who heard military sirens going off in some areas, seeing fleets scattering to the skies. And the broadcasts continued going out, one by one, all over the world.

In Omaha, several thousand marched on city hall. This touched off a spark that was the beginning of a simultaneous explosion. They were starting to march everywhere when Audipress, almost at dusk, finally responded to subscribers.

Commander Scott appeared on the screen. His gloved hands held a paper from which he read a statement. He said a few words, asking for order, and promising that full explanations would be forthcoming. What had happened was a calamity, the engineering of a small group of men whose purpose it was to undermine worldwide defensive forces. And he requested all citizens to await further developments peacefully.

Peacefully...

What the people had wanted was a denial—a complete denial. Even though many would never have believed it. Most people knew it was the truth, knew it was past denying, but they wanted a denial anyway. Explanations and talk of a small group of conspirators did little to ease tensions. And when word got out later that a combat ship had been sent to investigate the flimsy, meaningless message received from a Dr. Kimball Crane, that made no difference either.

In York, the huge square where Military Intelligence Headquarters stood among the government buildings, a great, horrible, squirming mass of humans descended and surged forward in aimless waves, overpowering guards, screaming their demands for the truth.

In Washington, two regiments held back a large mass of maddened people, nervously firing above the mob to keep them from reaching the White House grounds. In San Francisco, in Buenos Aires, Sydney, Cairo, London, Warsaw, Bombay, Yokohama…stark, staring craziness…

"Orders have gone out," said Audipress, "to all vessels to proceed only with volunteer crews. The full strength of the Interplanetary Military has been mobilized and is on guard. There is no immediate danger."

No one was listening or believing anymore.

At midnight on the American continents, a dozen cities were riddled with riots and flaming buildings, and other fires were beginning all over the world.

CAPTAIN Andrews stood on the rostrum of the combat ship, the *Solitary C,* in the crew assembly room. It was the largest single chamber aboard the vessel, yet the thirty odd men that had gathered there were crowded next to each other. Silently, the captain looked at the men of his command, his eyes pausing at the red field that encircled a service star on the uniforms of every man present. But for that red field he knew nothing about them, save perhaps young Lieutenant Rafferty, whom he had such a short time before found it necessary to discipline. It seemed a long time ago now.

The captain had been speaking for almost ten minutes before he had stopped. He cleared his throat and pulled on his little mustache, the mustache that would twitch involuntarily whenever he moved. He looked for a fleeting instant at Rafferty, then at Lieutenant Anthony Brown, and as he looked at both men, his eyes grew smaller, as though distracted. He finally moved on.

"That's the way things are at home," Captain Andrews continued. "I've told you everything Headquarters sent over the etherphones. The whole thing has blown up. Our duty, whatever value it may have, seems more clear than ever. We were ordered almost three days ago to a rendezvous, and we are now almost at our destination. That it may prove dangerous you know fully as well as I do; your red fields prove that. One thing more. M. I. has ordered that we proceed only with volunteer crewmembers. In view of the information that I have given you, everyone of you is at liberty to request release. I will wait for your decisions."

The captain turned on his heel, left the rostrum and exited from the assembly room.

A quarter of an hour later, Lieutenant Rafferty walked into the captain's cabin.

"The list of those who wish to resign, sir," he said. He laid a folded sheet of paper on the Captain's desk.

Andrews nodded, picked up the sheet, and studied it briefly. Quietly, without looking up, he said, "We've come a long way in these few days, haven't we, Lieutenant? Funny the way things worked out. The lad with too much vitamins being here with me now." He brushed a hand across his forehead and opened the sheet again. "I'll say this while I've a mind to, Rafferty. I got my red field in my first year, too. I was glad to take active command again, and I'm glad you're with me on the *Solitary C.*"

The next moment he laughed dryly.

"Look at this," he said, pointing to the sheet of paper.

Rafferty looked. There was one name: Lieutenant Anthony Brown.

Rafferty said, "Does this mean we must return to an outpost and allow Lieutenant Brown to leave the ship?"

The intercommunications phone piped twice.

"Observation reporting. Steinberg needle behaving erratically. Nothing visible."

The captain pressed down on one of the ivory buttons on his desk, then picked up his phone.

"Check with the chief engineer and report back." He juggled the horizontal bar and pressed down another button. "Communications. Captain Andrews. Request Lieutenant Brown to come to my cabin, please." He laid down the phone.

"No, Rafferty," said the captain. "It doesn't mean that at all—in this particular instance. It would be unfortunate for the reputation of this ship if it had to return, being so near its ordered rendezvous." He lapsed into silence again.

A FEW moments later, Lieutenant Brown entered. He saluted and stood at attention. The captain eyed him, soberly.

"Mr. Brown, are you aware that you alone of this whole crew has asked to be relieved?"

"I am now, sir."

"You have, of course, excellent reasons for your request?"

"I have, sir."

"Would it be too much for you to tell me something about them?"

"I am under no compulsion to divulge personal affairs, sir."

The captain nodded.

"Correct, Lieutenant. At the same time, I find I must tell you that your request cannot be honored."

Brown stood quietly a moment. Then he said, "The orders were to be enforced without exception, sir. I must insist on my rights."

"You have no rights, Lieutenant," said Andrews, slowly. "I see that your post at Communications has been very educational to you. You seem to have deciphered even my orders. Were you a bit puzzled when that other message came in some ten minutes ago? Odd code, wasn't it? A very private code, Mr. Brown—orders from H. Q. to the commanding officer, alone." Brown didn't budge as the captain added, "Those orders were for your arrest, Mr. Brown."

"I don't understand, sir." Brown's large figure shifted ground.

"I don't either—yet. Not entirely. Although it seems you have—"

The intercommunications phone piped twice, interrupting.

"Observation reporting, Captain. Chief Masters speaking. Steinberg needle denotes presence of a vessel in the vicinity. Impossible to verify by sight."

"That's odd," said Captain Andrews. He started to rise when suddenly the *Solitary C* heeled over as if her sides had smashed against a great wall. The lights went out. The deafening thunder of energy bolts pounding the armor of the vessel came just as the ship went into a dive. A wall gave way and suddenly it was hot inside the room, the air scorching.

Rafferty, hurled against one of the walls, saw Captain Andrews as the emergency light flickered on and then off. The captain was near him, pinned to a wall—so was Brown.

"Rafferty!" the captain shouted above the din, "Rafferty! What the hell!" The look on his face was queer for a moment, like someone who really didn't know what to do. His voice then sounded in the darkness. "We've been attacked, Rafferty—bolts and heat guns!"

The artificial gravity of the ship was gone, and Rafferty felt himself pinioned against the walls by the force of the ship's descent. At least it felt like descent, like free fall. On all fours he made his way to a porthole. There was nothing to be seen. The velvet black of space was gone. They were whirling through a grayish, curling mist.

It was then that a golden figure flitted through a wall and went close to Rafferty, spinning in a wild motion. Over the deep, terrible sound of agony that shook the very structure of the ship and the screaming of men, Rafferty heard Brown's voice, shouting something.

From near at hand a greenish light began to glow, a beam as thin as a pencil, aimed directly at the golden figure.

In the last moments of consciousness, hardly knowing what he saw or heard, Rafferty rolled across the floor. His last motion was to reach the safety valve, opening the compressed air jets to cushion the landing of the disabled, stricken vessel…

CHAPTER EIGHT
"Keep Fighting!"

THE morning of June 11, as Steve calculated time, found Kimball Crane and Steve scudding over the ground in their ses saucer, moving swiftly over the wind swept fields some ten feet under them. Both men were haggard, their faces lined with fatigue. They sat slumped in the shallow vessel, their eyes fixed on the horizon, where the early sun had illuminated, with all its brilliance, a white city in the distance.

Crane pointed behind. There was another ses—or maybe a distant bird—flying behind them. Half an hour later, when Steve looked again, it was closer—and it *was* a ses. It kept gaining on them bit by bit—until Steve suddenly cried out and turned his own vessel about.

Tommy was in the other ses. They could make out his waving arms, and his voice came faintly through the wind.

The two vessels approached each other with increasing speed. They met in mid-air, hovering. Tommy was direct and to the point.

"Follow me."

He twisted his vessel in an arc and Steve followed. Both were moving at a right angle to the direction in which Crane and Steve had been moving.

Tommy looked as if he was ready to collapse from exhaustion at any minute. From between lips that were swollen with thirst he managed to make himself heard. Unlike Steve, whose face had become covered with hair when it was no longer necessary to hold the guise of a nottar, Tommy's face was clean shaven. And in the vessel beside him lay a robe made of blue cloth. He said, "There's been a round-up. Harvey and hundreds of other humans have been taken to the Tribunal. I went there and sneaked in, disguised as a bikko. They caught me briefly but I managed to get away."

It was difficult for him to speak. He breathed heavily for some time and then, moving his ses closer still, he said, "The cloth bundle—the Chain—it fell out of my robe…gave me away. The llanu have it now. So I came after you. I was actually at the white city ahead of you. I scouted around, looking for you."

"How in the hell did you get there before us?" Steve asked.

"My ses is faster than yours…" Tommy answered. "…a lot faster. But we've got to get back to the Tribunal. We must get Harvey out…"

"Hungry?" Steve shouted across to him.

"I forgot to take along the boranny meat," Tommy smiled back.

"We did too. But Crane and I bagged a couple of them yesterday." Steve tossed across a bag with the remains of the meat to Tommy's ses. "There isn't much left."

"You never leave much," said Tommy. "Had no time to hunt. Had to find you. No time to eat or sleep or anything. No time left." He was chewing savagely on the cold meat, gnawing the bones. "I've been to the white city and I saw what was there. Just a few days left at most. They're getting ready to move.

"Don't bother speaking," said Crane.

Tommy grinned again. "Easier to speak than think the words across. We gotta get Harvey before he's decerebrated."

"What did you see at the white city," Steve asked, leaning toward Tommy.

Tommy shook his head. "Haymes isn't around. Gone somewhere. None of his men around, either. Doc Bell was on the right track, though."

The walls of a city of rose and gold stood on the horizon.

"There it is…" said Tommy, "…home of the llanu Tribunal."

"Doc and I have been doing nothing but talking for two whole days and nights. Tell us more about what you saw in the white city…"

"Keep your mind on Harvey," said Tommy.

THE rose and gold colors on the horizon were speeding toward them. Some time later they made out a ses high above, carrying several people. Soon there were others. Tommy pointed to them and said.

"The human round-up continues."

Crane asked, "Is this the city where they keep the female *llanu?*"

Steve started to smile, then answered laconically, "Yeah. Females are a rarity on Amanas. Only the nottars and spregg have any, and we—like the bikko—haven't. Bikko don't have to reproduce, and they don't want any of the normal humans to for very good reasons. But the llanu males seem to outnumber the females a hundred to one."

"I imagine they'd fight a lot over them," said Crane.

Tommy smiled back. "Wait'll you *see* the females."

By then they were almost upon the city. The air about them carried no less than half a dozen ses, yet those aboard ignored Crane and his two friends.

They were passing over the first outlying buildings now. They were all either circular or ovaloid, and of varying heights in regular formations, but all of them had a great central opening, a wide, circular shaft that began at the roof and went down the length of the buildings. The lovely rose and gold walls had many circular windows that were open, and here and there Crane saw faces at the windows. But he saw no llanu anywhere. The verdant streets below were empty, and looking down an occasional airshaft, Crane saw ses moving in them, but no llanu.

"There aren't more than a million of them on the whole planet, all told," Steve interposed on Crane's thoughts.

Ahead, Tommy's vessel came to an abrupt stop. Steve followed suit. Below them in a marvelously ordered panorama whose colors were like the blending tones of an artist's palette, stood a building with multicolored spires reaching up from a roof that dipped toward its central opening shaft.

As if by a signal, both ses dropped like plummets straight down into the shaft. Down they sped through numerous flights, flashing by other vessels. From what Crane could glimpse, the interior reminded him of luxurious hotels on Earth. Most of the levels had no railing along their outer edges; a small curb ended the level and it fell into the shaft. Here and there were great chambers, tapestries. Several llanu walked about, and wheeled to look at them as their ses sang its way down.

Suddenly the ses eased off, stopped, and slid out of the shaft to a level whose edge was marked off by a high metal railing. But the ses didn't descend to the floor itself. It hovered in mid-air for a moment.

The level was planned as a series of long halls, which moved like radii from the center of the shaft out toward the walls of the circular building. Intersecting these at several places were other halls, complete circles concentric with the shaft, increasing in circumference as they were farther away. The chambers were marked off between these intersections. And the halls themselves were filled with people—humans!

THEY sat about in various positions, clad in diverse ways, entirely silent. Many bikko moved among them, soundlessly. That was the extent of what Crane saw as his ses began to float down one of the halls. More than anything, the silence struck him. The place was like a bright tomb, the brilliant walls and blue robes of the bikko making a gay picture.

"Harvey! Harvey! Where are you?" The voices of Steve and Tommy were like thunderclaps in the quiet as they shouted. One or two of the bikko leaped for the edges of their ses but fell short. They kept moving down a long hall. The humans looked up at them with no curiosity in their eyes.

Crane was beginning to feel the hopelessness of his situation. He knew the three of them might never leave this place alive. Better to end the useless struggle and resign themselves to an easy death? Crane pondered that as he sat idly in the ses and looked at Steve, wondering why they had come.

"Crane!" Tommy shrieked in a loud whisper, his eyes blazing. "Watch out for the llanu whisperers. Don't let them get you. Keep fighting. *Keep fighting!*"

With these words, Crane's mind was suddenly alive again. In a flash he saw the minute panels in the ceiling, and the eyes of llanu peering out. These were the eyes he had been looking at before, without knowing it, and these were the eyes that accounted for the strange stupor that claimed the humans who sat below like cattle—and the eyes that directed the bikko who were now pouring in from all directions.

The ses were moving faster now, and at the next intersection of halls Tommy veered away and proceeded down a different corridor while Steve chose another. Crane reached over and took the control knobs from Steve's hand.

"You look for Harvey," he said. "I don't know him by sight." Steve surrendered the controls to Crane without a word.

The bikko were leaping underneath in crazy, vapid-eyed groups. Both men could hear the sound of the bikko jumping, their feet patting against the floor. One of them latched on momentarily but was brushed off by a wall as the ses rocked from one side to the other.

Suddenly a door opened and a llana stood there ahead of them. He came forward rapidly. His giant hands moved up, seized an end of the vessel, and with prodigious strength, moved it down. Half a dozen bikko clambered in, seizing Crane and Steve.

It was hardly a fight, and to make it more simple, it had no sooner begun when Tommy's voice rang out from somewhere in the distance...

"I've got him!"

CRANE, standing on his feet on the floor, had chopped his way past an army of bikko, his arms going like pistons, scattering the lumbering bikko like ninepins. They went down in all directions, to one side, under him, even against Steve who was grunting beside him, likewise hammering down the blue-robed half-men that kept running up to them.

Two things stood out in Crane's memory later. One was the way the captive humans who sat on all sides didn't budge. They let themselves be trampled on, fought upon, and would not even flee to safety. They just looked on, vaguely, their eyes troubled, like so many stone figures. The other thing was the way the winged giant who pulled their ses down had acted—it was in the same empty-eyed manner. He simply looked on and did nothing when Crane and Steve fought their way past him. One blow from his mighty arm would have settled the whole insane affair. Instead the llana gazed quietly at the ongoing battle scene.

At the nearby intersection a fresh group of bikko was waiting for them, their bare arms sticking out from under blue robes like wrestlers' paws. Heads down, Crane and Steve charged them, plowing through like battering rams. Back into a radial hall they plowed, and at the end, standing against the high metal railing of the shaft, they saw Tommy.

He had his back against the shaft, and he was kicking out with both feet. The floor around him was alive with blue-covered bodies. Beside him stood a human clothed only in the bottom of a gray tunic. He was using his hands on the bikko with heartening effect.

In a few moments the four men joined forces. It was just as well because the bikko were coming on in increasing numbers. Crane felt his knuckles growing raw. Fatigue alone would defeat them unless they could escape—soon.

Tommy's ses was hovering in the central shaft unattended, and at their level. Tommy yelled, "Give me a lift, Harvey!" The man in gray stooped and boosted Tommy up to the edge of the railing. Tommy gained the top, stood in precarious balance for an instant, and jumped! His hands clutched onto one end of the craft. In the next instant, the weight of his body swung the ses around and got it closer to where Crane and Steve stood waiting.

But just as Tommy kicked out, his body dangling from the edge of the ses, one of the bikko reached out and grasped Tommy's leg. His tired eyes met Crane's, and he smiled a brief smile...

Then he let go of the ses!

Tommy hung for a minute face down, held by one foot. The bikko who held him opened his hand. Tommy then disappeared from view.

He plummeted down into the shaft.

"Tommy!" Steve called out in a frantic, grief-stricken cry, the echoes of his voice reverberating down the shaft...

Crane leaped to the top of the railing, swung one foot over and seized the ses. He maneuvered it out of the shaft, brought it right over the heads of Steve and Harvey, moved again, and let it drop. It fell with a sickening impact on the bikko around the two men. Swiftly, both men jumped and climbed into the ses. Crane yanked it back up, into the shaft, and started up. But just as the ses moved into the shaft, Crane glimpsed the sprawled figure of a body lying at the bottom of the shaft, two hundred feet below...

The ses kept climbing, up out of the shaft. It was free again.

Steve pointed a finger.

"Go that way...to the white city..."

HOURS later, toward dusk, the three men rose from where they had hidden themselves in a grassy knoll and climbed into their vessel. Steve spoke again for the first time in many hours.

"I always ate more than my share," he said. He covered his face with his hands and wept.

After a time Harvey put a hand on Steve's shoulder. Harvey was as tall as Crane, and two mild blue eyes looked out gently from beneath a head that was pure white.

"Steve," he said. "The Tribunal halls were filled with men like Tommy. We didn't know them. Tommy gave his life in the hope that there wouldn't be any more men like those. Any one of us would have done the same."

Steve looked up again, out across the horizon. He took the controls from Crane's hands and turned them.

"The white city is that way," he said.

Now, as the ses moved swiftly into the gathering dusk, Crane and Harvey spoke. There was no way now of knowing what information Tommy had about the white city. There was no way of knowing what he had discovered there.

They knew only, these three, that one of them was gone. They were resolved that he should not have gone for nothing. "Keep fighting…" he had said in that faint smile, the Tommy who had fought to the last.

The three men sped onward, not knowing what the next few throws of the dice would bring…

CHAPTER NINE
The Golden Coffin

"THE railing," Harvey was talking softly to Crane, "around the shaft on that level where we were, was designed to keep men from jumping in and killing themselves. They discovered long ago—on the Tribunal level—that it was necessary. Sometimes, while they were leading men from the Judgment halls to be decerebrated, there would come a lucid interval like an awakening, and men would dive into the shaft. The llanu didn't like it."

The time passed more quickly when they conversed with each other. There was nothing to do but sit and talk, and in that way perhaps to stop thinking. Somewhere along the way they had lost their supply of lilacs—the ridiculous lilacs and their strange chlorophyll potency—and it was better not to think about what might happen without them—when the night fell. So they made conversation.

"Is decerebration a common punishment?" said Crane.

"A defense, more than a punishment," Harvey answered. "Yesterday they began to bring in every normal human, no matter what his function, and despite apparent innocence. There must have been a thousand all told. I had been doing valuable work for the llanu as an irrigation engineer, helping them water several new types of trees, like our Lombardy poplars and sequoias. They had no real reason to take me in, and I'm sure they knew nothing of my past dealings with Steve and Tommy. It was just part of a general round up. Something big is in the air. Something's about to happen and they're taking no chances any of the normal humans on the planet."

"That substantiates what Dr. Bell—" Crane began, when Steve, looking over the side, held up a warning hand.

Below them lay the geometrical perfection of a city. Even in the darkness they could see the walls of pure white, their central shafts brilliantly lit, and the light escaping to point like bright fingers at the starry sky. Even at their height, and after Crane's experience in seeing the silent towers of the llanu, there was something more than mere quiet here. The white city was like the dwelling of death. The radiant lighting only emphasized the utter desolation. What had Tommy found here?

The ses was descending, avoiding the illuminating rays that poured from the center shafts, dodging like a huge bat in the darkness.

"Where do we go from here?" said Steve.

Suddenly all three men were tense. There was circular area ahead, an immense expanse of grassy terrain with a diameter of easily half a mile. The circumference of the circle was marked off by a band of phosphorescent blue.

"We can't stay here…" Harvey whispered. The blue was an invitation to death—

And the ground was moving!

182

FROM the middle of the circle, the ground was shrinking back, shrinking back from the center point, and where the ground moved away there was a black pit without visible depth. Back and back the ground kept retreating, shrinking away from the center.

A tiny light glowed deep inside. A white light, and its radiance seemed reflected in gold, shimmered faintly. The light moved. There was an arm holding the light. A human arm.

Silently the ses dropped. Down it went past the level of the ground, and still farther down, and as it dropped, they saw a man all alone, holding the light.

"Abe!" Steve said, trembling. "It's Abe."

Abe looked at them as they dropped down beside him. They quickly and quietly exchanged greetings.

"Where's Tommy?" Abe asked.

"Gone," said Steve, quietly. "What is this?"

"I found the cloth...the Chain...that Tommy dropped when he was here earlier. It said something about a ship being here in the white city—a ship that men might use. I was at the Tribunal posing as a bikko, and when they caught me, I was...uh...*helped* to escape."

"Who helped you?" Crane asked.

Abe ignored the question and continued. "I came here and found this pit open. A type of roof closed over me while I was looking around inside this chamber. And then it opened again moments ago."

"Tommy must have found it open," said Steve. "But the blue—we're exposed to it. Have you any of the lilacs, anything with chlorophyll?"

"No I don't—and that may be a problem for us. But look over here. I'm sure Tommy must have seen this, too." Abe stretched a hand out. Halfway out his bare arm stopped.

Under the palm of his hand a gold radiance began to form. There was something solid there!

Crane put his hand out. He felt a somewhat smooth surface, but with little indentations engraved in it everywhere. And as his hand came into contact with the smooth barrier, a golden luminosity came from within it.

Abe had put out the white light that came from the tiny ball in his hand. The only light now was the golden radiance from the barrier, glowing warmly around the hands of the men pressing against it. The light seemed to come from within, as if the barrier itself was no more than a shell.

As the brightness of the glow increased, it became apparent that the golden area they touched was simply part of an immense, spherical wall, curving upward many feet—and on the other side of that wall were llanu!

THEIR faces were old, and they were lying inside as if they were suspended in mid-air. They seemed to fill up every available inch of space that the men could see. There were many, many of them. It was all Crane could do to keep his hand on the sides of the luminescent golden barrier as he looked within.

It was no more than a huge golden coffin.

"Take your hands off," said Abe. His thin little face and his shaven head were waxen in the glow from the sides. The men took their hands away. The inner golden light faded. In Abe's hands the tiny white ball glowed again. He stood before them, a small man clad in the blue robe of a bikko, his eyes bright. "This light in my hands is a present from...from the llanu," he said.

"From the llanu?" Steve uttered, almost in disbelief.

But before Abe could say anything further, a rumbling noise was heard overhead. The three men looked up—the ground was moving together again over their heads!

Abe looked puzzled, but not alarmed. He turned back to the barrier and held the light over it. The outside was covered with writing, and as Abe moved the light to and fro it became apparent that the writing seemed of many kinds and in a great many distinct sections. The men followed Abe as he passed the light over different areas.

"Sanskrit," said Abe. "Next to it is ancient Greek. And here are symbols of a sign language comparable to those used by the prehistoric cavemen of Earth. And here is something like medieval German."

The entire surface was covered with various writings, and they seemed to have taken in the range of many languages—all Earthly in origin.

"Steve," said Crane, "is there any sign of the language of the llanu?"

"There may well be," Steve answered softly. "We couldn't cover this in a week. There may be modern English too, but where?" He was intently studying the section of medieval German. "I think," Steve said, after a moment, "that I can make some of this out—most of it, in fact."

Abe came closer with the light.

"You can?" he said, eagerly.

Steve nodded.

"I wasted plenty of time in college," he muttered. "They always had their own notions about what an education should consist of, but I did excel in the study of extinct languages. But I never dreamed I'd use it outside of those musty libraries." He was poring over the words, delicately engraved lines in the surface. "Some of those professors were just cracked enough to have looked forward to a situation like this," he mumbled.

"Out with it, man…out with it," Harvey said urgently. "What do you make of it?"

"Hold on a moment," said Steve. "Let me translate. *Viele jahren*...uh...here it is." He took a deep breath and began to speak slowly.

" 'COUNTLESS ages ago, the llanu lived on Earth, like a flower evolved from the primeval slime, nurtured into being by a Divinity. They blossomed and covered the world with their cities, for they were even in that early day civilized beyond dreams. They were happy, but their happiness unwisely bred in them an arrogance that was their eventual downfall.

" 'For a time of ice came to destroy them. Walls of ice began to form on the warm bosom that had borne them, and it moved closer to their cities.

" 'But the llanu thought to evade the chastisement of the Divinity. They were resolved to survive, and so resolved, they had planned in time to leave the Earth and return to it when the walls of ice had receded.

" 'Whereas before all their energies had been intent on themselves, they turned their eyes out upon the wondrous universe, seeking to bridge the void that lay between them and a safe haven. Their engineers set out to find a way to leave. Then, of all the universe, they found a heavenly body suited in atmosphere and size to their needs, with its own tiny sun revolving around it. This was the planet Amanas.

" 'They fled then, and saw their cities destroyed, while they waited in other cities prepared for them in advance. But when all the llanu had gone, still the ice would not recede quickly. The great experiment began.

" 'It was in answer to the great experiment that the hand of the divinity smote them again.

"'The llanu found that the planet Amanas was not, as they had thought, a fixed member of their universe. It had no fixed orbit at all. It was a wanderer, doomed to stray over the countless planes of Creation, from universe to universe, forever alone. And even then, the lamentation of the llanu was tempered by their arrogance. They would answer the Divinity with their great experiment.

" 'Then, for the third time, Divinity struck…'

"Lord," Steve said softly. "There's more here, sort of a prayer."

" 'We have wandered eon on eon, age on age. We are sad and humble. We long for the ways of our fathers. We have prayed unceasingly.

" 'Now, returned to Earth, Poros, the end of our sorrow, we know that our prayers have been answered. We give thanks. Life may again go on for us.

" 'Here in this vessel lie llanu waiting for peace. They will be the first to obtain it.

" 'Give thanks, reader, to the truth of the Legend, and be humble.' " Steve's voice stopped. There was no sound.

After a time Crane said, "This would explain why the vegetation here has been modeled after the Earth. They couldn't actually have grown any of our flora because this planet was from outside our solar system. They must have been in dark space for ages sometimes."

"More important," said Abe, "it gives solid body to the stories and legends of the Planeteers. If this planet has only gradually been creeping back toward Earth, that would explain why the stories began all those years ago. Years ago, when the llanu were still far away from our solar system, only those ships that ventured out near their planet were seized. But as Amanas came closer to the edge of our solar system, more and more ships wandered into its range, and the llanu seized all of those, too."

"You've left out Haymes," said Harvey. "Where does he come in?"

Before Harvey could answer, Steve said suddenly, "What are we all standing here for, asking ourselves riddles? Doc Bell said there was a ship of some sort that could return us to Earth. We've got to find out if there really is—maybe it's somewhere near here. But right now we're inside a place that's been cut off from the outside in some way—sealed over. We've got to find a way out." Steve paused and looked at Abe. "It doesn't seem to worry you, though, Abe. What are you holding back?"

As if to answer, Abe looked up into the vault of darkness. A fluttering of giant wings came to them—and there it was! A llana was slowly flying down to them!

WHEN the llana alighted in the glow of the white ball, Crane held his breath.

It was a female!

She was perhaps eight feet tall; her long blonde hair came over her shoulders in one thick strand. She was clad in a flowing tunic of pure white. Her eyes were soft and dark; her features composed a portrait that was beautiful beyond description; her figure was willowy and supple. She advanced to the men with firm steps.

Abe said, "This is what I was holding back. I promised not to mention her unless she revealed herself. Thela helped me escape from the Tribunal. She brought me here and gave me the white light. And it was she who closed the opening above as she guarded me from the Raie."

The beautiful Thela looked down at the men, her eyes searching their faces.

"Do you mean to help us?" said Steve.

There was silence for a moment. Steve said, "We do not all know your language. It would be better if we spoke in mine."

Then Crane heard the words, or knew them, as they were focused on his brain, and he knew that the llana was telepathising.

"In the morning I will help you to take this golden coffin. It will bear you to your native Earth. I do this not for you, but for the soul of the llanu."

"Why should we believe that you will do what no other llana would?"

"Many would, if they knew what I do. I am one of the few who knows that this coffin must leave within a scant few days. My father was one of those who built it. If you do not believe me I must find others who will."

"There are no others," said Steve. "Why must we wait until morning?"

"No others...? Then you must believe me. Unless this coffin leaves Amanas soon, chaos and death will come to your world. You must wait until morning for only then are the attendant Raie still for a time."

"Why do you call this a coffin? What does this all mean?"

"Have you not read the inscriptions? Do you not understand them?"

"No. We know only your origins. We know that you plan to re-take the Earth—Poros, the end of sorrow."

"There is so much you do not know. It is difficult for me to speak in your language. Listen to me in my own words. The Raie of the living llanu in this golden coffin are even now with our priests."

AFTER that, Steve stood with his eyes closed, his body swaying slightly back and forth. Crane heard nothing further in his mind. Thela appeared to be communicating with Steve only. Crane then put his hand on Steve's shoulder and felt the other's body vibrating in a feverish tremor. Crane himself was lost in thought. Thela had said that there were *living* llanu in what she had repeatedly called a coffin! What meaning was there to this? What was she telling Steve? Why was she even with them at all?

The silence continued warm and vibrant.

Suddenly the ground trembled so violently that the little glowing ball in Abe's hands fell from his grasp. It lay at their feet and outlined the men who stood there, poised and tense, as still as statues. Crane saw Steve open his eyes and stare steadfastly at the llana.

Then he turned and said, "She says a military ship has fallen to the ground near here. On board was one of Haymes' men, armed with a green ray. Haymes' ship is on the way right now, descending to the crash site."

"If that's true," Abe cried out, "we've got to get to that ship and take it for ourselves!"

Steve turned back to the llana. Then he said, "She won't let us go. We might not return, and there would be no one to help fly the golden vessel."

"I'll stay," said Harvey suddenly. "I'm the engineer here. If it means so much, I can remain."

A moment later Steve said. "Thela says it's all right if at least two of us stay, so Harvey, if we aren't back by the time the sun reaches down past the opening to this pit—leave! Abe, you stay with him. You're the only one besides me who knows the whole story, and you've got to get back to Earth to warn them. The Doc and I are going."

Crane was already waiting in the ses when Steve jumped in. They waved goodbye in the sharp white light, looking unreal as they ascended, half of them distinct, the other half cloaked in shadow. High above them the wings of the llana guided them.

The ses paused momentarily and the ground opened up above. Then they were through...

THERE was someone moving near Rafferty. He had been listening for minutes, not knowing whether to trust his ears. His eyes had been unable to penetrate even an inch of the pitch-black night that surrounded him, not knowing whether it was night or whether he had been blinded. Through the roaring in his mind, and the lashes of pain that swept over him, he had been listening to that soft, steady sound. Someone moving.

"Rafferty," whispered Captain Andrews' voice. "What happened?"

Rafferty didn't answer. His head was reeling again. He slumped back against something solid behind him, and he knew nothing more...

Then there was someone shaking him. His eyes opened. A minute might have passed since he had last opened them, for he was not blind—no, there was gray light coming into the ship, through gaps in the torn hull of the vessel. But he felt no pain. He gave up thinking about it, and his sight brought a figure into focus. Andrews spoke again.

"Rafferty, do you hear me?"

He tried to nod his head but didn't know if he had.

"Listen," said Andrews. "Listen closely..."

The sound of a radium torch came to them, eating into the metal of the ship. "Whoever it was that attacked us," said Andrews, whispering, "they're coming in. I heard the torches an hour ago."

Judd Rafferty moved his lips, and slowly he forced sound out of them.

"How many of the crew are alive?" he asked.

"I don't know. My right leg's broken. Those air valves saved us. Maybe they saved others. I think we struck the aft side first. We seem to be tilted."

Rafferty was pressed close to a wall. One of the chairs had broken loose and lay nearby; the desk hung by a hair. The nose of the ship was up in the air, tilted away from them. The torches then stopped all at once.

They could hear steps ringing inside the ship. The sounds were coming closer. Someone at the door. Rafferty saw two men come in, walking on the sloping floor with difficulty in spite of the heavy magnetic shoes they wore to keep their balance. They wore dark coveralls with no insignia, and they were armed with heat pistols. They looked at the two men who were lying on the floor, then moved to a third— Lieutenant Brown, who lay in a heap under the desk, out of sight.

"Dead," one of the men grunted, presently. There was a tiny pool of blood that neither Rafferty nor Andrews had noticed. It had trickled down the sloped deck to clot against a wall.

"All right," said the other. "Get the chlorophyll ray tube. And see whether these two over there have any guns."

"They'd have used them if they had them," said the first man, dryly. He stood up from his stooped position.

"All right...here's the tube."

He was holding a long, smallish tube that glinted silvery. Then he looked at Rafferty and Andrews.

"Give it to 'em."

Rafferty closed his eyes. He knew there might be a look in them to betray the man in dirty white clothes who had sneaked up and was now at the door, his fingers to his lips, gesturing for silence. It was Andrews' slight cry of surprise that gave it away.

BEFORE the two intruders had half turned around, the man in the doorway leaped down from his elevated perch. He smashed into the nearer of the two men and sent him sprawling into his partner, both men ending up on the floor. But they didn't stay off their feet for long. Whichever way they fell, the magnetic shoes kept straining to lift them erect again. The man in white was pounding away at both, struggling to keep their hands from their holstered weapons. And then Rafferty dragged himself over and took a hand.

One of the men in coveralls fell near Andrews, who grabbed for the man's arms. He held him for a fraction of a second, then let go and tumbled away. The air sang and grew hot and a tiny hole appeared in the chest of the man in coveralls. It sang again and after that the sounds of the struggle stopped. The second man let his arms go limp and he lay on the floor grotesquely, his feet standing, and his body curled over.

Steve stood in the doorway, a heat gun in his hand.

"Hated to spoil your fun, Doc," he said, "but time's short. If we'd bothered to look on the other side where these boys landed, we'd have seen their ses."

"Who are you two?" asked Rafferty, from where he sat.

"He's Steve," said Crane. "I'm Kimball Crane."

Rafferty's eyes misted, and he brushed a hand across them.

"Hello, Crane," he said, softly. "I got that first message you sent. Second one too."

Crane rose to his feet. "And who are you?"

Steve said abruptly; "Save your questions, gentlemen. If we don't hurry, there may be no use giving any answers. Let's get out of here."

Crane and Rafferty bent over to help Captain Andrews as he dragged himself across the deck.

Steve suddenly lingered behind. "There isn't anyone else alive outside of this room," he said, "but you might pick up a couple of these." He patted his heat gun.

"What are you lingering back there for?" Crane asked. "Let's get going."

"How many men do you remember Haymes having on his ship?" Steve asked.

"Maybe fifty."

Steve smiled a wan smile. "All right," he sighed. "Help those two out, will you, Doc? I'll be along in just a minute."

Crane raised and eyebrow at this but asked no questions.

Outside, Crane saw with a start that the sun had begun to climb into view. The time was slipping away fast. He helped the wounded officers into the ses and sat beside them silently, waiting for Steve. The two men in uniform looked about them with bewilderment, but said nothing.

Presently Steve emerged. He was dressed in the coveralls of one of the two dead members of Haymes' crew. In his arms he carried three large copper triangles.

"Rocket bombs," he smiled, cheerfully.

"What are you up to?" said Crane. "What are those clothes for?"

"You're right, Doc," Steve grinned. He held up a hand. "Don't try to argue. You'll only waste time." He came closer and held out a hand. "Look, Doc," he said. "Things have been happening to us, going our way. We've got to get that coffin off. Abe knows the reason why and he'll explain it to you. But somewhere near here is Haymes' ship. Somebody's got to make sure he doesn't spoil things. These little rocket bombs are a swell guarantee."

Crane said slowly, "Steve...you aren't coming with us?"

"I'm part of the guarantee," Steve grinned.

"Can't let you do it, Steve," Crane said flatly.

Steve started to say something as Crane took his hand. He never said it. Crane's left arm saw to that. His fist flashed out and caught Steve flush on the jaw. Crane frantically caught his body before it could hit the floor.

"That was close!" Crane exclaimed, "I hear these bombs go off easy."

He took the three rocket bombs from Steve's clutching hands and laid them gingerly on the ground. Rafferty and Andrews looked on in astonishment.

"Don't need any guarantee," Crane said as he carried Steve's limp form to the ses. He opened one of the pockets in the coveralls and saw the silver tube in it. Then Crane touched the knobs and the ses lifted. Crane was mumbling to himself. "Did he think I'd let two of the best men I ever knew die here?" Crane was angry at the thought.

MANY minutes passed before Crane saw the great circular area in the white city. He sat now soaked in his own sweat, his jaw grim. He had been long in finding the city. Steve and he had flown around aimlessly while trying to locate the fallen ship and he had lost all sense of direction. Steve was coming around, slowly. Crane's punch had had a much stronger effect than he intended.

And where the hell did I get that kind of strength? Crane asked himself.

The circle in the deserted city was before him now and it was closed. The sun had barely touched its outer white ring that had the night before glowed with intense blue. It appeared that the Raie within were inactive. If Crane derived any humor from his situation, it was from watching Rafferty and Andrews as they gazed with astonishment down below, seeing Amanas and knowing absolutely nothing about the planet.

Crane was soon directly over the center of the circle.

"How am I going to get this thing underneath the ground?" Crane muttered softly to himself. As he spoke, he saw Rafferty looking at him queerly.

Then, as Crane exchanged looks with Rafferty, he laughed. Rafferty's eyes were popping open. The ground beneath was moving away like the iris of an optical instrument, drawing within itself. The huge pit under the ground grew larger and larger. It was then Crane's turn to stare down in disbelief.

The golden vessel that everyone had called a coffin was more gigantic than Crane had realized. The first rays of the morning sun glanced off the top of it and made a dazzling sight.

The ses descended toward the outer edge of the pit, then Crane saw something else: The golden vessel lay in some kind of massive declivity that was now filled with a bubbling liquid—*and it was slowly rising out of that liquid.* The night before, Crane suddenly realized, it had been mostly submerged in that declivity, and they had only seen the upper portion of it. Even as he watched, the vessel kept on rising, slowly but steadily. Then Rafferty gave out a startled cry. His arm was pointed upward...

The sky was suddenly filled with ses!

There were dozens and dozens of them, laden with countless bikko. The men could then see they were accompanied by hundreds of llanu, who dotted the sky in between the descending bikko craft. They were still a distance away, but there was no doubt they were heading straight toward the golden vessel.

"They're coming to stop us," Crane cried.

When Crane's ses touched the ground, he jumped out. Was the golden vessel leaving without them? Where were Abe and Harvey? Then he saw them...

Inside the vessel!

They were staring out grimly at him. They were plainly visible, as was every little detail of the cubicle in which they were standing. The rest of the vessel had a golden transparency to it, and everything within was visible—there were many thousands of llanu, seemingly dead, and seemingly suspended in mid-air. It was an astonishing sight.

Crane then saw Harvey reach to an instrument-studded panel and run his hands over it. The golden vessel stopped moving. A small door opened near Abe and a platform walkway descended over the top of the bubbling liquid, touching the ground a few feet away from the awe-struck men.

"Come on!" Abe shouted.

"The llanu!" Steve shouted back, pointing upward.

Abe glanced up—his face when dead white. "Hurry!" he screamed.

Rafferty was standing dazedly in the ses, looking around him. Steve took him by an arm and helped him out. Crane stood for a moment surveying the bulk of Captain Andrews, then with a grunt he stooped over and lifted him to his shoulders. He carried him inside the golden vessel behind Steve.

"Got everything?" Harvey asked from within.

Crane scowled. "Yes! Get us out of here...now!

Harvey pulled a switch. But there was no sound. The liquid underneath seemed to boil over and then the men saw the pit receding slowly. And then—as they watched the many llanu and bikko craft hovering helplessly outside their vessel—they began to ascend with ever increasing velocity.

"Some boiler," Harvey grunted, looking at the panel.

They were on their way...

CHAPTER TEN
The Heroes

"WELL," said Abe, and he picked his teeth slowly. He enjoyed talking to such an interested audience. "Well," he said again, looking from Crane to Rafferty to Andrews, and then at Harvey and Steve who were playing a game of dice by themselves, "what Thela told us is going to haunt my sleep for the rest of my life."

Crane looked wearily out of the side of the vessel, out into the placid black depths of space. Captain Andrews had estimated, together with Harvey, that they still had at least another day to go. It would probably take Abe that long to finish telling his story.

"To hell with your sleep," Crane said with no feeling.

Abe sat up. "It's a strange story," he said, seriously. "It began with the early days after the llanu fled the Earth. They believed that their Divinity had punished them first by bringing the glaciers. The second blow came when they discovered that Amanas had no fixed orbit and was a wanderer.

"Then they started what they called their great experiment. In short, it was a search for immortality—but it was also a search with a purpose. They wanted to live to return to their native Earth.

"It was an empty dream, of course, and it was never fulfilled by the original llanu scientists who had concocted the whole scheme to begin with. But even after many generations had gone by, the original scientific work still went on. Slowly, through scientific means we can only guess at, the life span of the llanu was lengthened until it had become almost two thousand of our years.

"It was a triumph, of a sort," said Abe, his voice growing softer, "but the llanu paid for it as no living creature has ever paid. That was what they meant by the third blow of Divinity…"

"What do you mean?" Crane asked.

"They ceased dying normally as they once had. At first it happened to only a few—a ghastly state of "undeadness." But then it spread quickly after that. Soon the majority of the llanu were faced with a time when their bodies were too feeble to live—*and yet they would not die!*

"There had to be an end to all things, even as there had been a beginning. They were not divine. But when their bodies ceased functioning, their spirits, or life-force, left them, free of the body, wandering entities that sought relief from agony and restlessness."

"What do you mean?" said Crane, frowning, "their *spirits?*"

Steve spoke up. "He doesn't translate it well, Doc. Thela referred to these spirits as the Raie. She explained it as 'Lotii-Bey.' It means more or less 'the life force,' the essence of being, the spark of life. They believe the Creator kindled that spark, and that when the body died, the spark was extinguished. But in this case, even after their bodies ceased functioning, that spark lingered on."

"Their beliefs can't explain concrete phenomena," said Crane. "Did these Raie have substance? What were they?"

Abe shook his head. "You know as much as we do. *You saw them,* and I did, too. We saw them kill. We know they exist, whether as spirits or ghosts or as specific scientific entities that could be labeled perhaps as balanced forms of pure energy. They must have had substance, or we could not have seen them. But what they actually were, we must accept the word of the llanu. Their Raie have been with them for millennia upon millennia.

"WHAT about their prophecies—the ones whose inscriptions are carved into the surface of this vessel?" asked Crane.

"I was coming to that," said Abe. "The llanu race had to return to Earth, and some day they would. They believed that. It was the foundation of their religion. They were haunted by the agony of their protracted death process. All the while that their bodies lay expiring—so slowly expiring—the Raie of the body wandered in agony, shrieking, miserable, seeking death and the peace of death. The curse of that death decimated them. When the llanu originally fled the Earth, they numbered in the billions. There are now, according to Thela, less than a million. The llanu refused to breed, refused to bring children into a world that made their exit from life such a horror. They saw mockery even in the golden tint that edged their wings as they grew older, for soon that golden auro was visible in the Raie. The Divinity was mocking them, they said.

"They had to enact laws to force breeding. Even then, there were female llanu who undertook their own suicides rather than comply. There is now a far smaller percentage of female llanus than male. Eventually the llanu religious hierarchy, knowing what the death of the body meant for the soul, decreed that no llanu could kill anything, regardless of its age, or even take such action as might result even accidentally in death."

"But why did they want the Earth?" asked Andrews.

"Their Legend promised them that once they had returned to Earth—and in that way they would know their Divinity was appeased—that from that day on they would again die normally and end their lives in the manner of all Earthly beings. Then would come release from all sorrow.

"And then, some two hundred years ago, Amanas came near Earth again after what seemed an eternity in deep space. The llanu knew salvation was at hand. The Legend had said that if they returned, the Raie would find peace. But after the llanu discovered what the Raie could do to human beings, they determined that the Raie would be the force used to re-take Earth."

"You mean," said Rafferty, "that they would allow the Raie to kill humans?"

"They killed," Steve interjected, "but it was more than that. The Raie seemed to be able to suck out the life of a human. There was nothing really wrong with the remaining human bodies, you understand, but the spark of life was simply gone. The Raie would vanish after that. The llanu said that they affected a union with the human spirit, and that this human spirit—or life force—upon going to its peace swiftly, would take along the Raie and give them a swift peace, too. Every time a Raie attacked a human, when the human died, the Raie died too—finally. That was the main reason why Haymes returned to Amanas when he brought Doc Crane. His Raie had all been exhausted on the *Flambeau* and he wanted more. To him the Raie were weapons."

"HAYMES, we know now," said Abe, "made the discovery that chlorophyll was a poisonous substance to the Raie. Why it was poisonous is hard to explain. Thela said, as we long suspected, that the balance of potential energy in chlorophyll—which one might call a spark of life—would destroy parts of the energy balance within the Raie. If chlorophyll was near, it somewhat compromised the power of the Raie and merely caused them to transfer living entities from one to another instead of destroying them. But Haymes found a way of harnessing the power of chlorophyll into small silver tubes that emitted a type of chlorophyll-based energy ray. With this he had a weapon that could destroy the Raie. That's how he controlled them and kept them from destroying his crew."

From the corner of his eye, Crane saw Rafferty suddenly jump up.

"The silver tube—the green ray—we forgot it!" Rafferty cried.

"Not true," said Crane easily, patting a large bulge in his pocket "Got it right here. I retrieved the tube from Steve's coverall pocket after I decked him."

"I've wondered about that," said Andrews. "When you knocked Steve out, how did you know we wouldn't need to use those rocket bombs he was carrying against Haymes' ship?"

"I didn't." Crane seemed cautious in his answer. "It was a spur-of-the-moment calculated risk. I figured that whatever llanu vessel we used to return to Earth in—as it turned out, this golden vessel—that it was a good bet it would be well protected, probably even invulnerable, from attacks by Earthly weapons, including the weapons on Haymes' ship. I guess I was right, because we surely would have been blown to smithereens by now. Besides, would Haymes really have attacked a sacred llanu ship after conspiring with them?"

"And I guess Steve hadn't figured that out when you slugged him," Andrews observed.

"No," Crane replied.

But what Crane didn't mention was the real reason why Steve hadn't wanted to return to the white city with them. Steve had wanted to stay behind with Tommy. Steve had been with Tommy so long it hardly mattered to him whether he lived or died. Crane wanted to avoid mentioning it. Steve had to go on living.

Crane heard a whisper then...a whisper in his mind:

"Thanks, Doc."

Crane smiled, as he winked across the cubicle to Steve.

"Where was I?" Abe was saying. "Yes, the weapon. Well, Haymes got this tube to keep the Raie at bay altogether. With his discovery of the llanu, the Raie, and Amanas itself, he now had what he'd gone into space to seek—vindication! And Haymes also penetrated the veil of invisibility with which the brilliant engineers of Amanas had cloaked it,"

"Is that why it's never been visible through Earth telescopes?" Harvey asked.

"Yes," Abe continued, "and Thela tells us that Haymes first discovered Amanas by following the Raie who were floating in space near the planet. He must have incurred losses amongst his crew, though, before his discovery of chlorophyll as a defense.

"Haymes soon became a man of enormous power. For he was, in a sense, invulnerable to the llanu, who could not kill him, nor could the Raie! On the other hand, Haymes could not only kill the llanu with ease, but he could ruin all their plans by returning to Earth and revealing their strategy to the world. The llanu, bound by eons of rigorous religious belief, could not kill him or any of his crew—even in self-defense!

"Now Haymes had a choice to make, and he chose the road to madness. His soul must have been sufficiently embittered by then. He made an alliance with the llanu. He would help them take the Earth, if they granted him certain favors later.

"What favors," Crane asked.

"We're not sure. Thela says that the idea of an alliance was repugnant to the llanu, but they couldn't really refuse. Haymes could not live forever, and he would prove a valuable, if ruthless, partner when they moved against Earth. In other words, he did their dirty work for them. Year after year the llanu had taken humans to Amanas from space vessels. Thousands became bikko, some were fodder for the Raie, and a few of them were assigned to certain tasks, like Harvey. But soon the normal ones had grown too strong in knowledge. Steve's group, of which I was one, were all men who knew about the power of the chlorophyll in the lilacs. With this as a defensive weapon, we were essentially beyond the power of the llanu or the Raie. So Haymes was brought in to subdue us. He murdered more than five hundred of us. Of the others who ran away, some were eventually caught by Haymes—when hunger or the whisperers or loneliness hadn't beaten him to it.

"What about Brown?" Andrews asked.

Abe nodded and continued. "Haymes also planted a team of his men on Earth to leak the story of an impending threat from space. He wanted to cause a panic and disrupt the

Earth's defenses in lieu of the forthcoming invasion by the llanu and the Raie. Brown was part of that team. Haymes certainly succeeded in this regard."

"BUT there were rebels, heathens, also among the llanu. They were those who believed that our common origin was a sign from the Divinity. They wanted to share the Earth with us, not exterminate us. They helped the normal humans whenever they could and kept fighting the plan of the llanu majority. We hoped that it might lead to a chance for us to escape. It never did.

"The break we needed came almost too late. I ran across Dr. Bell at the Tribunal. He'd been tricked into giving his number and was taken by the llanu. I passed along the information I got from him to Steve. He and Tommy then went out in search of the Chain. And the Chain told us two things. One, that there was an enormous ship that Haymes had helped the llanu build—in the white city."

Crane got a perplexed look on his face. "I've been thinking about that, Abe. Why was it left unguarded?"

"I can only assume the llanu felt there was no need for security. After all, the ship was completed and lying in readiness. It was scheduled to take off, with the accompanying Raie, within a few days. They had also rounded up—or so they thought—all normal humans they perceived as being a threat. The ship was supposed to leave in the middle of June, to bring death to the Earth, by bringing with it the Raie of countless dying llanu. However, Bell didn't know at the time why the date had importance to the llanu. We figured that out later."

"Why *was* the date so important?" asked Rafferty.

Abe looked at him thoughtfully and said, "Amanas has come as close to the Earth as it will ever come—*and it is just now beginning to wander away again!*"

There was complete silence as Abe stopped speaking. His lips were dry. He reached over to the water flasks and poured some out.

"We're running short of water," said Harvey.

"Good water too," said Abe, taking a deep breath. "Thela was wonderful. She supplied this ship with enough food and water for the journey back to Earth. She also gave the white-light ball to me. It was a special gift she said. She spent half the night explaining it to me. And do you know what she was going to do after we left?"

Rafferty shrugged his shoulders. "Not a clue, Abe."

"Give herself up to the Tribunal for punishment. That's religion, I say!"

"Still no sign of Haymes' ship?" asked Andrews.

"No," said Steve. "The Doc was right. He won't follow us. If he could have stopped us he certainly would have by now."

"Abe," said Crane, at length. "You mean the planet Amanas is retreating back into the void?"

Abe took another drink from the flask, nodded solemnly, and smacked his lips.

"Amanas is returning to the depths of deep space. This was a now or never chance for the llanu. In truth their plans wouldn't have ever really succeeded, but they would have caused great trouble for the Earth. Thela believed if we flew the coffin away without the attending Raie that it would end the threat until Amanas was too far away for them to try again. And she was probably right.

"You see the llanu undoubtedly had no idea how much chlorophyll-based life forms there were on Earth, nor how many billions of humans there really were. Oh I'm sure the Raie could have caused all kinds of death and mayhem, especially in the towering sections of Earth's major cities where there is little or no chlorophyll present. But ultimately there would have been just too many humans and way too much chlorophyll for the dwindling population of the llanu to contend with."

"Why wouldn't have Haymes clued the llanu in on all this?" Rafferty asked.

Craned jumped in at this. "Because ultimately Haymes probably didn't care whether their 'sacred' invasion succeeded or not. In his twisted mind he wanted two things: revenge against his home planet...and proof positive to the people of Earth that everything he had written in his book, *Inquiry,* was true."

What about the llanu in this ship?" Harvey asked. "What's going to happen to them when we reach Earth?"

Abe shrugged his shoulders. "Let them die peacefully and give them a decent burial I suppose..."

"And their Raie?" Harvey shot back.

"Who knows," Abe answered. "Doomed to eternal damnation perhaps."

"So we're floating home in a coffin," Rafferty observed in a solemn tone.

"In almost every sense of the word," Abe continued. "It is filled with thousands and thousands of dying—yet not completely dead—llanu. For some reason the Raie cannot venture too far out into space unless they're within the confines of a spacecraft or accompanied by their dying llanu bodies. To go to Earth, the Raie would have to have these bodies transported there with them."

"Then the Raie still could be with us?" Rafferty asked, a slight touch of apprehension in his voice. "Outside this ship...hovering near us in space?"

"NO," said Abe. "We got a jump on them. We saw the bluish forms of some of them trying to follow when the vessel was still in the white clouds of Amanas, but the Doc took pot shots at them through the weapons portal until they were all gone. You and Andrews were still a bit under when this was happening."

"Worked fine," Crane admitted with a grin. He fondled the silver tube in his hands and put it back in his dirty white tunic.

"He's a good shot, the Doc is," said Abe.

AN hour later they were quarreling in high spirits.

"The hero of the expedition is the Doc," said Steve. "He and his mighty left hook pulled us out of many a tight spot."

"Nonsense!" said Harvey. "No disrespect for that left hook, Doc, but where would we be now without that silver tube? The arrival of the M. I. patrol—there are your heroes."

Abe grinned. "I'll take Thela, not forgetting that the Doc here sent deep space messages twice to the M. I. to get them clued in to what was going on out here."

Crane began to speak softly. "Some of the heroes of this expedition were left behind us. They were the men like Tommy and Doc Bell. Also men like Abe and Steve, and every human who gave his heart and mind and blood to the fight, many of whom are no longer recognizable as normal humans, but we here know what they did. Our answer was a common one, achieved by many men. Even here in this vessel, we have begun to think of how interdependent we were. We may think of the countless interweavings of events as chance—but there were men who made those chances, who fought for them. Each tiny link was vital. Without one link—even without the traitorous Lieutenant Brown who followed the orders of Haymes with those others who brought unreason to the world—even without that link, there would have been a common failure…"

Kimball Crane looked out of the side of the ship. It was a coffin that carried the sorrow and travail of a doomed race.

The dying llanu were in that ship, far from their foster-parent, Amanas. Their world was each day dying. It was drawing away again, to wander forever as a planet of ghosts. Each day would see it farther and farther away, and their existence would one day be a Legend, engraved in the sorrows of mankind, in the death they had brought, seeking their own salvation. It was the law of all life.

And Haymes? Doomed to spend his days on Amanas, or as a frightened and hunted outlaw.

Crane had heard of what had happened on Earth. He knew that he was to see people who had recently been living in fear of unknown terrors; to look at cities razed by panic, some areas even in flames; to hear tales of horror and death. But he knew that he would see them build again and live again.

The Earth was a huge round form that filled a quarter of the heavens from where Crane sat. It was beautiful to see.

THE END

Made in the USA
Coppell, TX
04 February 2025

45431586R00122